W9-BSV-519

BREAK POINT

What Reviewers Say About
Yolanda Wallace's Work

The War Within

"*The War Within* has a masterpiece quality to it. It's a story of the heart told with heart—a story to be savored—and proof that you're never too old to find (or rediscover) true love."—*Lambda Literary*

Rum Spring

"The writing was possibly the best I've seen for the modern lesfic genre, and the premise and setting was intriguing. I would recommend this one."—*The Lesbrary*

Murphys's Law

"Prepare to be thrilled by a love story filled with high adventure as they move toward an ending as turbulent as the weather on a Himalayan peak."—*Lambda Literary*

Visit us at www.boldstrokesbooks.com

By the Author

In Medias Res

Rum Spring

Lucky Loser

Month of Sundays

Murphy's Law

The War Within

Love's Bounty

Break Point

Writing as Mason Dixon:

Date with Destiny

Charm City

BREAK POINT

by
Yolanda Wallace

2015

BREAK POINT

© 2015 By Yolanda Wallace. All Rights Reserved.

ISBN 13: 978-1-62639-568-8

This Trade Paperback Original Is Published By
Bold Strokes Books, Inc.
P.O. Box 249
Valley Falls, NY 12185

First Edition: October 2015

THIS IS A WORK OF FICTION. NAMES, CHARACTERS, PLACES, AND
INCIDENTS ARE THE PRODUCT OF THE AUTHOR'S IMAGINATION OR
ARE USED FICTITIOUSLY. ANY RESEMBLANCE TO ACTUAL PERSONS,
LIVING OR DEAD, BUSINESS ESTABLISHMENTS, EVENTS, OR LOCALES
IS ENTIRELY COINCIDENTAL.

THIS BOOK, OR PARTS THEREOF, MAY NOT BE REPRODUCED IN ANY
FORM WITHOUT PERMISSION.

CREDITS
EDITOR: CINDY CRESAP
PRODUCTION DESIGN: SUSAN RAMUNDO
COVER DESIGN BY SHERI (GRAPHICARTIST2020@HOTMAIL.COM)

Acknowledgments

Tennis and history have always been two of my major passions. With this book, I was able to combine both interests. *Break Point* was inspired by the lives of two tennis greats—Baron Gottfried von Cramm and Alice Marble.

Modern tennis fans often call the 2008 Wimbledon final between Rafael Nadal and Roger Federer the greatest tennis match of all time. Tennis historians, however, consider the 1937 Davis Cup match between German Baron Gottfried von Cramm and American Don Budge to be even greater. The stakes were certainly higher in the earlier match than the one that came seventy-one years later. When Nadal and Federer squared off, only a Grand Slam title and professional pride were at stake. When von Cramm and Budge faced each other, the result was practically a matter of life and death.

Californian Alice Marble was one of the pioneers of serve-and-volley tennis. She was also one of the few female players in the 1930s who dared to wear shorts on court. Her affairs with men and women were well-known, but her role as a spy during WW II remained a closely guarded secret until she revealed the details in her 1991 autobiography.

Though *Break Point* is a work of fiction, I tried to make the characters and the often dire straits in which they find themselves as real as possible. Please be sure to let me know if I have succeeded.

As always, thank you to Radclyffe; my editor, Cindy Cresap; and the rest of the BSB team for making the publishing process so enjoyable.

I would also like to give my sincere thanks to the readers. I appreciate your continued support as well as your feedback. Keep those comments coming!

And last but not least, thank you, Dita, for always being in my corner. Game, set, match.

Dedication

To Dita.
In tennis, love means nothing. Since I met you,
however, it has meant everything.

CHAPTER ONE

September 1937
Berlin, Germany

"Next stop, Alexanderplatz." The customs agents roamed the narrow aisle with passport stamps dangling between their ink-stained fingers. They had come on board after the train crossed the border between France and Germany and had been making their way through the long string of cars ever since. "Please have your papers ready for examination before the train reaches the station."

Meike von Bismarck, Germany's most accomplished amateur female tennis player, gathered her belongings. After a storm-tossed week-long ocean voyage from America, followed by a bumpy train ride from Paris to Berlin, she was ready to relax for a few days and spend time with friends before she began the final leg of her journey. A relaxing car trip in the passenger's seat of her friend Friedrich's new Rolls-Royce Phantom, a gift from a wealthy male admirer, would take her home to her family's lakeside estate along the Swiss border. But home could wait. First she wanted to spend some time in one of her favorite cities in the world.

Friedrich, the most renowned—some would say infamous—drag performer in Berlin, had warned her the city wasn't the same as it once was, but she hoped he was exaggerating as he was often wont to do.

In its heyday, Berlin was home to hundreds of nightclubs catering to gay men and lesbians or adventurous liberals looking for a good time. Lesbians could live openly, but gay men had to be much more discreet. Nevertheless, gay men were so popular in certain circles, they were practically fashion accessories. No night on the town was complete without a visit to one of Berlin's notorious gay bars, which featured something for all tastes. From classy cabarets where the dress code was strictly black tie to more rough and tumble establishments featuring live sex shows on any or all of multiple floors.

But that was before. Before local police stopped looking the other way. Before Paragraph 175 and the Nuremberg Laws made sex something to be kept secret instead of celebrated. Before the Austrian came to power.

"Your papers, please."

Meike reached into her handbag, pulled out her travel documents, and handed them to the customs agent who had asked to see them. The agent checked the documents a bit too thoroughly for her comfort, then, betraying his military background, clicked his heels and returned the papers with a slight bow.

"Welcome home, Miss von Bismarck."

"Thank you. It's good to be back."

Despite the long voyage, Meike disembarked the train with a bounce in her step. She loved being able to see the world, which her tennis career allowed her to do, but nothing could take the place of home. The region she had grown up in had remained unchanged for hundreds of years, but she couldn't say the same for Berlin. Her heart sank as she realized Friedrich was right. The city that had once beckoned artists and writers with its promises of freedom now felt like the capital of a police state.

The train station was a beehive of activity, but, except for the employees, the people in it were ominously quiet. Black-uniformed SS officers and scowling youths in brown shirts and matching trousers cowed everyone within their purview into submission, their steely eyes daring anyone to question their authority. Returning and departing passengers with downcast eyes and wary expressions scurried to their destinations like children trying not to raise the ire of an overly strict parent. The scene made Meike wonder if she had stayed away too long or if she hadn't stayed away long enough.

She watched as a family of three—a man, a woman, and their young daughter, a wisp of a thing in pigtails and a sack-like jumper she had yet to grow into—were paraded through the station by a cadre of armed guards. The woman's hatbox, which was clutched under one guard's arm, bulged with rolls of badly concealed Reichsmarks.

Attempting to smuggle money out of the country was a serious offense in cash-starved Germany. Even married couples who forgot to remove their wedding rings before they left the country were subject to stiff fines. If found guilty, the frightened family Meike was seeing now would undoubtedly receive an even harsher punishment.

She tipped a porter a few marks of her own to place the six large steamer trunks she had lived out of for the past three months into temporary storage. Then she continued on her way, a bit more cautiously than before.

Gripping her weekend bag in one hand and her tennis racquets in the other, she exited the train station. Outside, she shuddered, not at the steadily dropping temperature but at the sight of the swastika-emblazoned red, white, and black flags flapping in the breeze. Seeing the symbol of the National Socialist Party never failed to strike fear into her heart. Seeing so many of them lining the street made her wonder yet again about the direction her country was headed. How could so many of her countrymen choose to remain silent when millions of their compatriots were being slaughtered or left to die in the concentration camps that were springing up all over Germany? Were they afraid for their lives or were they too busy celebrating the economic turnaround that had finally put an end to years of rampant inflation to question the tactics of the man responsible?

Despite the public's good spirits, war seemed almost inevitable. Meike wouldn't have thought it a few years or even a few months ago, but the house painter from the tiny village of Braunau Am Inn had whipped a military still recovering from the lingering effects of the previous global conflict into a bloodthirsty frenzy. They hungered for land, money, and power. Shielded by the trappings of nobility, Meike and her family would be safe. But how many others would be able to say the same? How many of her friends and former lovers would fall victim to Adolf Hitler's hatred-fueled ambition?

Meike flipped up the collar of her overcoat to shield her face as she began to walk toward Friedrich's apartment. After Gottfried von Cramm's bitter defeat against American Don Budge in the Interzone Final of the Davis Cup a few months before, she had assumed the mantle of Germany's biggest sports star. She hadn't lost a match in more than two years and was the two-time defending champion at the French Championships, Wimbledon, and the US Championships. If she won any of those three majors in 1938, she would be able to retire the trophies, the originals gifted to her at the end of the tournaments, as well as the smaller replicas. And if she managed to win all four majors, she would no longer be a star. She would be a legend.

But this was no time to plan her pursuit of history. This was no time to be recognized. This was a time to be anonymous.

As soon as she reached Friedrich's apartment, she could stop worrying about who might be watching or what they would say if they reported her to the authorities. She could be herself, not Hitler's propaganda tool. Until then, she had to make sure she wasn't being followed so her friends could be safe from possible arrest.

She and her closest friends were gay in a country in which such a thing was not only frowned upon but forbidden. No matter which in a series of possible charges they received if they were caught following their hearts instead of the law, the sentences they earned would be swift and harsh. Hard labor, forced military service, or even death via an execution carried out on the spot.

Not wanting her friends to be punished for what they—and she—could not change, Meike decided to take a circuitous route to Friedrich's in the hope that anyone trailing her would lose contact or interest or both before she reached her destination.

"Countess von Bismarck?"

The two men weren't wearing uniforms, and the one who spoke tried to strike a friendly, conversational air, but Meike knew they were Gestapo as soon as they fell into step beside her.

She wanted to run even though she had done nothing wrong. Not in her eyes anyway. The Austrian and his accursed inner circle, on the other hand, might beg to differ.

"Meike or *Fraulein* von Bismarck will do." She hoped her smile seemed genuine rather than forced. She wanted to appear more relaxed than she felt. "The title of countess belongs to my mother."

Together, the agents looked like living embodiments of the number ten. One was tall and thin with the wiry build of a track athlete. The other appeared to have spent a few too many days sitting behind a desk. His ample stomach stretched the seams of his ill-fitting suit, and his breathing was labored, even though they had walked only a few meters from the station's entrance.

The thin agent placed a hand on Meike's arm as if they were old friends. "But that is what your fans call you, isn't it? The Countess?"

"Only on the court, not off." She stared at his hand until he removed it. "Do I know you?"

"No, but I know you." He reached into the inside pocket of his jacket, pulled out a packet of Turkish cigarettes, and lit one with a practiced flick of his thumb against the barrel of a stainless steel lighter. "I've followed the results of all your matches in the newspapers and on the radio," he said through a thick cloud of smoke.

"Thank you. I appreciate the support."

She tried to convince herself the man and his friend were nothing more than ardent fans, but her eyes searched the busy street for possible escape routes nevertheless. But if she did manage to get away, where could she possibly go? If the men were secret police, they would know everything about her. Who her friends were. Where they lived and worked. Who they loved. Who *she* loved. Her sexuality wasn't an issue as long as she kept winning tennis tournaments—she was too valuable an asset to the Reich to be hauled off to prison—but she didn't want to get anyone she cared for into trouble by leading the wolves to their doors.

"If you will excuse me, gentlemen."

Clutching her racquets to her chest as if they would protect her from harm, she turned back toward the station. Toward the safety of home. She would get word to Friedrich somehow and tell him she had decided not to stay. She would tell him what he probably already knew. Berlin wasn't safe for people like them.

The portly agent stepped in front of her, impeding her progress. Though he didn't speak, his intentions were clear. She was being detained.

"Step aside." Meike hated how ineffectual her voice sounded. She tried to summon the imperious attitude her mother so easily assumed whenever she was displeased, but she couldn't manage the feat. "Let me pass."

Although the portly agent's sweaty face reddened, he didn't move from her path. "I'm afraid we can't do that, *Fraulein*. We have our orders."

When the thin agent grabbed her arm a second time, his touch was no longer friendly. His grip was vice-like as he directed her toward a nearby car.

"What is the meaning of this?"

She kept her voice low despite her rising indignation. And fear. She didn't want to cause a scene until she knew what to expect.

The thin agent opened the back door of the idling Mercedes-Benz. Two more agents sat inside. Unlike their counterparts, they were wearing uniforms. Meike could smell the oil from their shiny leather boots. She could see the guns holstered to their sides.

She tried to tell herself the Austrian needed her—her celebrity, her accomplishments, and her blond hair and blue eyes made her the poster child for the so-called perfect race he was trying to fashion by extermination—but she feared the latest in a series of unexplained disappearances was about to be hers.

"Come with us, *Fraulein* von Bismarck," the thin agent said. "The *Führer* wants to see you."

❖

November 1937
New York City

Helen Wheeler woke with a start. The hammering in her head matched the rhythm of the pounding on her hotel room door.

"Open up, kid. It's me."

Helen recognized the voice of Swifty Anderson, her agent and favorite whipping boy. She derived great pleasure from giving Swifty grief, but she owed him her life. If not for him, she'd be stuck in Monterey, California, packing sardine cans for a living like the rest of her family instead of waking up with a champagne-induced hangover in a penthouse suite at one of the swankiest hotels in New York City.

In school, she had been an average student with average grades. Nothing special. Then Grace Johnson, her physical education teacher, put a tennis racquet in her hand, and she had gone from average to exceptional. Her family hadn't supported her new and rather expensive hobby, but Mrs. Johnson had recognized her potential and devoted untold time, money, and energy to getting her tennis lessons and driving her back and forth to various tournaments.

Helen won her first state title when she was fifteen, defeating a string of competitors who had been playing the game much longer than she had. By the time she was eighteen, seeing her face splashed on the sports pages of local and state newspapers became a common occurrence. Then Swifty had come along, talking fast and promising her everything under the sun. Six years later, her cannery row days were behind her, everything Swifty had promised her had come true, and the riches he had always said would be hers were almost within reach. All she needed to do was sign her name on the dotted line.

She freed herself from a tangle of shapely limbs and champagne-stained sheets, threw on a robe, and padded barefoot to the door.

She let Swifty in before he could start that infernal pounding again. "What gives? It's too early for even the roosters to be up, let alone humans."

"Haven't you heard? New York is the city that never sleeps."

Swifty was impeccably turned out as usual in a snap-brimmed fedora and a tailored suit. His shoes were polished to such a high sheen they shined even brighter than the sun rising in the early morning sky. Not for the first time, Helen wondered if he gave her all the under-the-table expenses the US Lawn Tennis Association sent her way or if he pocketed a sizable portion of them for himself. No matter. In a few months, she wouldn't have to worry if he took a slice here or there because she would have the whole pie.

"I had a breakfast meeting with a racquet manufacturer who heard you're planning to turn pro next year. They want to sign you to a deal before one of their competitors beats them to it. It's a good deal, but we can do better. I think you should hold out until something better comes along."

"And if it doesn't?" Helen hated the thought of leaving money on the table. Especially money that could disappear before she had the chance to claim it.

"Trust me. It will. You're the second-ranked female player in the world and the top American. Promoters are clamoring to sign you."

Helen rummaged through the discarded bottles of champagne until she found one that had more than a few drops left inside. "It feels good to be wanted," she said, pouring herself a glass.

"I'm sure it does, but I didn't come here to talk business." Swifty snatched the champagne glass from her hand and downed the contents in one shot. "There's a fed downstairs waiting to see you."

"What kind of fed?"

"The kind that asks a lot of questions but doesn't give any answers. Which means you need to make yourself presentable and I need to show your friend the door."

"Which one?"

Swifty took a second look at the bed and let loose with an appreciative whistle that cut through Helen's head like a buzz saw. "Jesus, kid. You saw more action in one night than I've seen in a lifetime."

"They say it's better to be lucky than good. Fortunately, I'm both."

Swifty rolled his eyes. "And so humble about it, too." He gathered the clothes littering the floor and tossed them on the bed. "Wake up, girls. The party's over."

The women Helen had met at the Cotton Club the night before—a high society type and one of the dancers from the revue—grumbled in protest.

"Chop, chop," Swifty said. "I don't have all day."

He reached into his pocket and pulled two sawbucks off a fat roll of bills. Hush money to insure Helen's nighttime activities didn't land her in the early editions of the next day's papers.

Helen wanted to have fun and enjoy the perks that came along with stardom, but she knew she had to be careful. Because of her working-class background and her brash, take-no-prisoners personality, some members of the press had it in for her. The same reporters who kept their pencils tucked behind their ears when they witnessed male athletes being unfaithful to their wives and girlfriends wouldn't hesitate to take pen in hand if they ever got the goods on her. For them, sports was an all-boys' club and she had dared to crash the party.

She had been dubbed "Hell on Wheels" because her temper sometimes got in the way of her talent. Despite her reputation as a hothead, though, she had won the Australian Championships three years running, and she had ascended to number two in the world rankings, right behind the unbeatable—and the unflappable—Meike von Bismarck.

Unlike Helen, Meike stayed cool when she played, earning her legions of fans around the world. Both in the press box and in the stands. Helen would miss going head to head with her, but she wouldn't miss always coming out on the losing end.

Meike's winning streak stretched back over two years. Helen had always thought she would be the one to break the streak, but the only thing she seemed destined to break was her own heart. No matter how hard—or how many times—she tried to pick up the pieces.

Swifty ogled Helen's guests as he watched them dress. Helen tried to remember their names. The high society type was Persephone and the dancer was Peaches. Or was it the other way around?

"With the amount of ice around the blonde's neck," Swifty said, "she should be paying me instead of the other way around."

Persephone—Helen was almost positive the moniker belonged to her—smoothed her beaded dress over her narrow hips and plucked the twenty from Swifty's outstretched fingers. "Cab fare," she said with the same haughty air that had drawn Helen's attention to her in the first place.

After she stashed the money in her clutch bag, Persephone stood and waited for her cheek to be kissed. Helen dutifully obliged. Persephone reminded her of someone. Someone her head had told her to forget. Too bad her heart had never gotten the message.

"Do call on me the next time you're in town." Persephone's voice dripped with manner and decorum, two things Helen had taken great pleasure in making her forget the night before. "Only next time, lose the unfortunate fellow in last year's suit."

Helen smiled at Swifty's obvious displeasure over Persephone's comment. He prided himself on always having the latest and greatest of everything so she knew how much Persephone's wisecrack stuck in his craw. "You can count on it."

"What about me?" Peaches asked in a sultry purr.

Helen took the second twenty from Swifty and slipped it between the lovely brown breasts she had spent several hours admiring initially from afar and, finally, up close. Then she took Peaches's hands in hers and pressed them to her lips.

"I'll be sitting in the front row for your next show. If you aren't careful, you'll high kick me right out of my chair."

"No chance of that." Peaches playfully batted Helen's nose with the tip of an ostrich feather fan. "My mama always warned me to watch out for sweet talking men, but she never told me women had silver tongues, too."

"Tell your mama my tongue's pure eighteen carat gold, baby."

Peaches let loose with a girlish giggle Helen hoped wouldn't harden into something more jaded in the years to come. Chorus girls had short shelf lives at the Cotton Club. They were put out to pasture after they turned twenty-one. Peaches had just turned twenty-one for the third time. She couldn't go on lying about her age forever. She could probably find work as a hostess or a cigarette girl, but Helen suspected she wouldn't be truly happy unless she was up on stage flashing those gorgeous gams. The memory of having those legs wrapped around her made Helen want to spend a few more hours in bed. Then Swifty cleared his throat to remind her she had business to attend to.

She had almost forgotten about the mysterious visitor waiting to see her. She wondered if their meeting would result in only a minor inconvenience or a serious roadblock. But first things first. She couldn't begin the day until she put an end to last night. And what a wondrous night it had been. One that had almost made her forget about the past. Almost.

Peaches's long, athletic dancer's legs nearly came up to Helen's neck. Helen stood on tiptoe to give Peaches a kiss on the cheek. "I look forward to your next performance."

"Not as much as I'm looking forward to the one you're about to give downstairs," Swifty said under his breath.

Helen gave him the stink eye as she walked Peaches to the door. If he kept flapping his lips like that, the twenty could turn into a down payment instead of a payoff. "Why does a fed want to see me?" she asked once she and Swifty were alone.

"I don't know. You tell me. You didn't sleep with someone you shouldn't, did you? On second thought, don't tell me. The less I know, the better. I don't want to wind up in the slammer because I had the inside dope that you showed the wrong dame a good time."

"If that was the case, her husband would be coming to see me instead of the feds, and I doubt he'd take the time to set up a meeting first."

She took a shower while Swifty looked through her things to find something suitable for her to wear. Most of her clothes were designed to be worn on the tennis court or out on the town. She didn't own anything sedate enough for a powwow with a government official.

As she dried off, she wracked her brain to try to come up with a reason why Uncle Sam had sent someone to meet with her, but she couldn't think of anything. Yes, she had accepted appearance fees and inflated her expenses, but she couldn't think of a single "amateur" who didn't. When she turned pro in a few months, she could be open about the money she earned for her skills. She wished she could be just as open about everything else. If she tried, though, the flood of sponsors who were courting her now would dry up like the Midwest during the Dust Bowl. She hadn't fought to survive the Great Depression just to fall short now that the good times were finally back.

When she came out of the bathroom, she noticed Swifty had selected an outfit that made a nun's habit look wanton. She picked up the white hat and matching kid gloves she hadn't worn since last year's trip to London for the Wightman Cup, the annual competition between teams of British and American female amateur tennis players. The US had won six years in a row, and she'd had a hand in four of those victories.

She liked winning tournaments, but she loved being part of a team even more. Winning was so much sweeter when she was competing for her country instead of herself. The biggest regret she had about turning pro was not being able to play in next June's inaugural Confederation Cup, a weeklong contest that would pit teams from eight countries against each other on the slow red clay of Roland Garros, the annual site of the French Championships. The most important team competition in men's amateur tennis was the Davis Cup. Next year, women's amateur tennis would finally get its equivalent. And she was going to miss it. But, depending on how her upcoming meeting went, deciding between professional and amateur tennis might soon become the least of her concerns.

"Should I be nervous?" she asked as she began to dress.

Swifty shrugged and turned his back to give her some privacy. "Like I said, you tell me. I would go with you, but he gave me the impression he wanted to meet with you alone. After I make the introductions, I'm sure I'll be eighty-sixed."

As usual, Swifty wasn't too far off the mark. After the hotel's elevator operator let them off on the first floor, Helen took Swifty's arm as they walked across the lobby.

"There he is."

Swifty whispered the words out of the corner of his mouth, but he needn't have said anything. With his carefully parted hair, square suit, and run-down shoes, the fed stuck out from the well-heeled New York crowd like a sore thumb.

"Miss Wheeler, I am Agent Paul Lanier." He flashed his badge so quickly Helen wasn't able to tell what agency he was supposed to be representing. "The hotel manager has graciously permitted us to use his office so we can talk in private. If you will follow me, please."

Helen tightened her grip on Swifty's arm. "I would feel more comfortable if my associate, Mr. Anderson, were allowed to accompany me."

Lanier arched an eyebrow at her request but didn't offer to fulfill it. When he adjusted the coat draped over his arm, Helen noticed the briefcase he was carrying. She didn't know what was inside, but she doubted the case was filled with endorsement contracts requiring her signature.

Swifty freed his arm and gave Helen's hand a reassuring pat. "I'll be in the bar if you need me, kid."

"Whatever you plan on ordering, make mine a double."

In the manager's office, Lanier sat behind the desk as if the room and everything in it belonged to him. Helen flinched involuntarily when he opened the locks on the briefcase with a snap.

"Relax, Miss Wheeler. I'm not here to harm you," he said with a smile that was probably supposed to convince her to trust him but accomplished exactly the opposite. "In fact, I came here today to ask for your help."

Now she was even more confused. "Unless you need tennis lessons, I can't think of any way I could possibly be of help to you."

Lanier reached inside the briefcase and pulled out a thick manila folder. He began to look through the folder, but kept it angled away from her so she couldn't glimpse the documents inside.

"The Federal Bureau of Investigation performed a background check on you last year when you agreed to put on a series of exhibition matches at US military bases at home and abroad at the First Lady's request."

Helen remembered the tour fondly. She hadn't earned a dime—the expenses she had incurred crisscrossing the United States and Europe for three months at Eleanor Roosevelt's request had outweighed the paltry stipend she had received—but the appreciative looks on the soldiers' faces had been payment enough. Even though the matches were meaningless and the only thing at stake was each player's competitive pride, the audience had cheered like they were watching Helen and her opponents compete in the final of a Grand Slam event.

"The questions you were asked were routine," Lanier continued, "but your responses were far from it."

Helen couldn't recall saying anything out of the ordinary during the extensive question-and-answer session, but something in her file had apparently captured the feds' attention. Otherwise, she wouldn't be sitting here having to explain herself to one of them.

"It says here you have a photographic memory," Lanier said. "Is that true?"

"Yes. Even if I read pages and pages of information, I can memorize them word for word in a few minutes' time."

The skill could have come in handy when she was in school, but most of the time she couldn't have been bothered to read the assigned material at all, let alone memorize it.

"Your ability—and your notoriety—could be very useful to us. No one would ever suspect you of being a spy."

Helen's heart lurched. She felt like she was acting out a scene from a dime novel. Only the plot Lanier was laying out was even more ludicrous than the one found between the pages of any book she had ever read.

"You want me to be a spy? Do I look like Mata Hari to you?"

Lanier didn't answer her question. Instead, he asked one of his own. "It's safe to assume you're familiar with Meike von Bismarck, yes?"

Helen couldn't understand the change in subject. Why was a federal agent asking her about Meike?

"I should be familiar with her," she said warily. "She's the main reason I've never been ranked number one in the world, and she beat me in the finals of Wimbledon and the US Championships this year."

Lanier shuffled the papers in his hand, drawing Helen's attention to them once more. "You used to have a relationship."

The word "relationship" took her by surprise. She was so mesmerized by the game of Three-card monte Lanier was playing with the documents in the folder she nearly responded to his statement honestly instead of tactfully.

"We used to be doubles partners, if that's what you mean."

She didn't know what truth he was trying to uncover. Was he going after Meike or was he going after her? Her carefully worded response might not have been the answer he was looking for, but it was the only one she was prepared to give.

"The two of you made a formidable team. Why did you end your partnership?"

He made it sound like she and Meike had been married an[their union had ended in the stigma called divorce. To be honest, that's what it had felt like when Meike had sat her down and told her they needed to go their separate ways. On and off the court. Fooling around with Peaches and Persephone and the dozens of women preceding them had helped to fill Meike's absence from her bed, but Lanier's questions reminded her how much she missed waking up to see Meike's familiar face across the pillow instead of the string of women she was able to forget almost as quickly as she was able to get them undressed.

"She said she wanted to devote herself to her singles game."

Even though the explanation had seemed logical, Helen had never been able to completely accept it. She had always known being the best was important to Meike, but she had never expected her to allow remaining number one to take precedence over everything—and everyone—else in her life. Until Meike cast her aside.

Lanier continued to flip through the documents in the folder, piquing Helen's curiosity even more. Was he ever going to let her see what he was looking at or would he continue to keep her in the dark?

"Based on her results, I'd say she made the right decision. She plays the occasional doubles tournament with Liesel Becker, so she hasn't given up the discipline entirely. Perhaps it would be more accurate to say she gave up on you."

"I appreciate the history lesson, Mr. Lanier, but I'm getting tired of being given the runaround. Are you a tennis fan, sir, or simply a fan of Meike von Bismarck's?"

He smiled wryly. "I wouldn't call myself a fan. I'm more of an interested observer. And I'm very interested in why Meike von Bismarck has been having private meetings with Adolf Hitler." He finally stopped perusing the documents in the folder and focused his attention squarely on her. "I'm also interested in when women's doubles became a contact sport."

her the folder with a quick, sudden gesture that
of an impulse than a planned action. Helen was
the move she nearly dropped the folder on the
ne regained her composure, she flipped the folder
open to find dozens of pictures of a grim-looking Meike entering
and exiting a building identified in neat black type as the Nazi
headquarters in Berlin. In some of the photos, Hitler himself
accompanied Meike to her waiting car. But those pictures didn't
interest Helen nearly as much as the ones of her and Meike.
Laughing over a bottle of Chianti in Rome. Dancing cheek to
cheek in London. Kissing in Paris like tomorrow would never
come.

She ran her thumb over an image of a smiling Meike dressed
to the nines at a drag show in Berlin. Friedrich, dressed as Jean
Harlow, was by her side. Though he looked like the spitting
image of the movie star, his artificial beauty paled in comparison
to Meike's natural wonders. Golden blond hair, bright blue eyes,
and a smile that made you feel warm all over every time she
flashed it in your direction.

The first time they'd met, Helen thought Meike was the most
beautiful woman she had ever seen. She still did. The second-
rate imitations she had tried to replace Meike with after their
parting didn't hold a candle to her. So why had she been foolish
enough to let her go without a fight? To save face for being the
one who got dumped instead of the one doing the dumping? Or
because she was all too used to being rejected by someone she
loved? First her family, then Meike. Though they had different
reasons for cutting her loose, it all came back to the same thing:
she wasn't what they wanted her to be. Their loss. Because she
wasn't going to change who she was. For anyone.

"What do you want?" she asked. She didn't bother to
deny what the second set of photographs meant. Pictures
spoke a thousand words and the pictures in her hands spoke for
themselves.

"I want your help. Hitler's keeping it a pretty piss poor secret he's rearming Germany's military, even though doing so breaks the treaty his predecessor signed at the end of the Great War. He has his eyes on Austria. Probably Poland and Czechoslovakia, too. What Uncle Sam needs to know are his plans for the US of A. Does he plan to get us involved in his mess or does he intend to leave us out of it? Should we be more selective about which foreign nationals we allow to enter the country, Meike von Bismarck included?"

Helen couldn't believe her ears. "The US Championships are held in New York. She's the defending champion. You can't deny her entry."

"Can't we? Why would we willingly allow a known enemy agent on our shores?"

"We aren't at war."

"Yet. Germany hasn't officially declared war on us or issued any formal threats, no. That's why I can't involve anyone employed by a government agency. I need someone who can act in an unofficial capacity. That's where you come in. If you accept the assignment I'm proposing, you would have a chance to clear Meike's name as well as your own. You're used to keeping secrets and you're not above telling the occasional lie to keep those secrets safe."

Helen bristled. "It's no one's business who I sleep with except for the person in bed with me, Agent Lanier. Telling a few white lies about my personal life in order to protect my privacy is one thing. What you're suggesting is another. I'm not a spy. I wouldn't know where to begin. What do you want me to do, travel to Berlin and ask Hitler what his New Year's resolutions are? I'm afraid he and I don't travel in the same social circles."

"But you and Meike von Bismarck do. She's part of Hitler's inner circle. If he's confiding in her, perhaps you can get her to confide in you. You were close once. You can be again if you play your cards right."

Helen winced at the thought. The last time she and Meike had laid their cards on the table, she had gone bust. She carefully placed the folder on the desk, distancing herself from what was inside.

"Meike and I won't be seeing very much of each other in the future. I'm joining the professional tour next year and she plans to remain an amateur. Her family's loaded. She can afford to play for free. I can't."

"You could have fooled me."

Lanier looked around as if to remind her of the luxurious surroundings in which they currently found themselves. The chandelier in the lobby probably cost more than he made in a year. He placed his folded hands on the manager's desk and leaned toward her. Though his demeanor was placid, Helen instinctively gave ground.

"If the government asked you to remain an amateur, would you be willing to change your mind about becoming a professional?"

Helen glanced at the manila folder. The photos were tucked safely out of sight, but the images had already been burned into her memory. "I get the feeling I'm not allowed to say no."

"It's a free country," Lanier said, "but everything comes with a price."

And it was time for her to pay up.

CHAPTER TWO

December 1937
New York Harbor

The *Southern Star* groaned with effort as it pulled away from the pier. Thick clouds of acrid black smoke poured from the stacks as the workers in the boiler room far below the water line piled on the coal. After a brief layover in New York City to take on more passengers and replenish the supply of both food and fuel, the ocean liner was continuing on its way to Adelaide, Australia. The trip would take forty-two days altogether. The ship was scheduled to arrive at its final destination on the eleventh of January, ten days prior to the start of the Australian Championships. Plenty of time for Meike to recover from the arduous transatlantic journey and adjust to the drastic change in temperature before the tournament began. January meant winter in Europe but summer below the equator. And Australian summers were like none she had ever experienced. She hoped she wouldn't wilt in the heat.

She hadn't seen the full list of expected entrants for the Australian Championships, but the tournament was a major so she expected the field to be competitive despite the sweltering weather conditions. A bit of friendly competition preceded by several weeks at sea was exactly what she needed to take her mind off her troubles.

Fingering the telegram in her pocket, she watched impassively as the newly arrived passengers lined the railings to wave at their loved ones on shore. Hats, handkerchiefs, and scarves flashed the semaphore of farewell.

She had no one to see her off on this leg of her journey. Friedrich was still at risk in Berlin, but her parents were safely ensconced in the family castle. They were safe because she was here. Far away from them and all the ones she loved. She couldn't stay away forever, though. She had to return home eventually. But where was home exactly? And what kind of life would she be returning to? Her country was no longer her own. It was in the Austrian's hands now. And so, unfortunately, was she.

"Perhaps you would like to come inside, Miss von Bismarck, and escape the chill."

She stiffened at the sound of Oskar Henkel's voice. The SS agent had been pulled from Heinrich Himmler's protection detail and assigned to accompany her to Australia. To insure her success or hinder it, she wasn't sure.

He was a pleasant enough fellow, if you found blind loyalty attractive, but she hated the very idea of him. She didn't need to be watched every moment of the day or shadowed by a man for whom she felt nothing but contempt, but this was her life now unless she bowed to Hitler's will.

If she joined the Nazi Party and competed under its flag, the restrictions on her would be lifted. As far as she was concerned, the restrictions could remain. The colors she wore when she competed were not the red, white, and black of the Nazi flag, but those of her tennis club, usually represented by the blue and gold ribbon she wore to keep her hair out of her eyes.

As much as she hated Oskar's unwanted presence in her life, she was willing to accept it in order to retain the principles she held dear. She would rather lose her privacy than her sense of self.

"In a moment, Oskar," she said with false cheer. "I won't be much longer. And please remember to speak English for the duration of our journey unless you want to give yourself away. Some of the passengers might think you're planning an invasion. It would be a shame if you were to be arrested before you were able to file your latest report. We wouldn't want that, would we?"

Oskar's thin lips briefly compressed into a frown as if he weren't accustomed to having a woman tell him what to do. Meike could tell he detested the assignment his superiors had given him. One of the very few things they had in common. She had lodged an official complaint with the German Tennis Association, but the tennis officials were just as powerless to combat the Nazi political machine as she was. Perhaps even more so.

She felt certain she could find refuge somewhere if she decided to speak out against the Nazi regime, but what about the people who weren't able to travel as freely as she? Without an escape route, speaking their minds could mean a death sentence. Her compatriots' silence didn't signify agreement as she had once suspected. For some, it signaled self-preservation instead.

"As you wish."

Oskar clicked his heels and bowed slightly before he departed. Even though she could no longer see him, she could still feel his eyes on her. Watching. Always watching.

She was used to having the eyes of fans, coaches, and fellow players upon her, but this was different. Oskar wasn't looking for flaws in her game but in her character. Any sign of weakness would be reported to his superiors and used against her. Used to try to force her to bow to the collective will. She was determined that scenario would never occur, but how long could she hold out? She was one person battling an entire administration. The odds were decidedly not in her favor. But losing was not an option. Not when losing could cost her everything.

She longed for the sanctuary of a tennis court, where good shots were rewarded, bad ones were penalized, and the rules didn't arbitrarily change to benefit one player and harm another.

She wrapped her fur coat tighter around her as the icy wind blew across the bow of the ship. Logic told her to retreat to the warmth of her stateroom—she didn't want to risk coming down with a cold that might deepen into pneumonia and cost her a chance at competing in the Australian Championships for the first time—but being surrounded by thousands of strangers made her feel free, a feeling she didn't know when she would be able to reproduce after she returned to Germany.

Her fingers closed around the telegram in the pocket of her coat and the words of comfort offered on the crumpled, tear-stained page.

MISSED YOU IN BERLIN STOP REGRET YOU HAD TO LEAVE SO SUDDENLY BUT UNDERSTAND WHY YOU HAD TO GO STOP GOOD LUCK IN AUSTRALIA STOP STAY SAFE UNTIL WE SEE EACH OTHER AGAIN STOP LOVE FRIEDRICH FULL STOP

Poor, sweet Friedrich. He was one of her closest friends. He had been ever since they met as children at the Rheinsteifel Tennis Club more than twenty years ago. She worried about his well-being even more than she did her own. By his reasoning, more people recognized him as a woman than as a man so he would be safe walking the streets as himself. So he had decided to stay. In Berlin. In Germany. In a country whose leaders no longer valued his existence.

Recently, he and several of his fellow performers had had their cabaret cards revoked, which meant they were unable to work in their chosen professions. Most of the others had fled to safer locales. Friedrich had friends on the French Riviera who had offered to take him in for as long as he needed refuge, but he had chosen to remain in Germany. Since he was Jewish, he couldn't leave the country without leaving ninety percent of his assets behind. He wasn't willing to add his hard-earned money to the Nazis' already bulging coffers. So he stayed, risking his life in order to make a stand.

Friedrich's bravery made Meike feel like a coward. Instead of standing her ground, she was running away. Hoping a change of scenery would improve her outlook if not her prospects.

She felt trapped. Caught between a world she once knew and one she wanted nothing to do with. She didn't know if she would survive the struggle or become yet another carefully catalogued statistic.

"A penny for your thoughts."

The accent was American, the voice hauntingly familiar. The sound of both stirred an unexpected longing in Meike. She turned to find Helen Wheeler standing behind her, a pleasant grin on her face and her curly brown hair blowing in the breeze. Even though it had been only a few months since they had played each other in Forest Hills in the final of the US Championships, to Meike, the match felt like a lifetime ago.

"Save your money," she said. "My thoughts aren't that valuable. What are you doing on this voyage? I thought you had decided to join the professional tour."

"And I thought you never ventured south of the equator. The Australian Championships have always been my stomping grounds. You already own the other three majors. You couldn't leave one for the rest of us?"

Helen's brash fits of temper on the court always made Meike cringe, but her cheeky sense of humor off it never failed to make her smile. "You didn't expect me to make it easy on you, did you?"

"Never."

Helen's gray-green eyes sparkled as her smile grew wider. Her eyes changed color according to her mood. Green meant she was happy, gray meant she was upset, and a mingling of the two meant something else entirely. Meike had been fortunate enough to witness all three.

"Is Mr. Anderson with you?"

"Swifty? He's around here somewhere. Before I gave him the slip, he was trying to set up a poker game with a group of swells so he can separate them from their dough. He'll find me eventually. I can't walk two steps without his clod hoppers stomping on my heels. Sometimes I feel like I'm Fay Wray and he's King Kong tearing the city apart trying to find me."

Meike knew exactly how she felt.

"You are, without doubt, the only person in the world who calls Swifty 'Mr. Anderson.' No wonder he likes you so much."

"I thought his fondness for me was due to my uncanny resemblance to Greta Garbo."

Meike felt herself begin to relax for the first time since she'd been taken to see the Austrian two months before. Then Oskar spoke up, putting an abrupt end to her brief respite.

"Miss von Bismarck, I really must insist—"

"Coming, Oskar," Meike said, unable to keep the exasperation from her voice.

"Who's the muscle?" Helen asked with a disapproving frown.

As far as Meike could tell, Oskar knew absolutely nothing about tennis, so she couldn't exactly say he was one of her coaches, but how was she supposed to explain his presence in her entourage?

"This is Oskar Henkel. I'm not sure of his official title, but his unofficial function appears to be making sure I don't have any fun."

Oskar's naturally ruddy complexion turned even more flushed as he bit back his anger over not having his order blindly obeyed. She was a citizen, not a soldier. She responded to requests, not commands.

"Well, we can't have that," Helen said. "Have dinner with me tonight. I'll make sure you have more fun than you can shake a stick at."

Pleasant memories flooded Meike's mind. Memories she thought she had forgotten but now came rushing back as if she were experiencing them for the first time. Memories of Helen's skin sliding against hers, warm and welcoming as Meike's body, in turn, urged Helen to find her way deeper inside. Memories of their lips and tongues coaxing one another higher and higher until they eventually crested and fell spent into each other's arms. The kind of memories she might not be able to make again. With her life in such turmoil, how could she possibly invite someone into it? Everyone she knew was already in danger. She didn't want to put anyone else at risk, whether friend or lover or someone who had once been both.

"Thank you for the invitation, Helen."

Oskar took Meike by the elbow and gave her arm a warning squeeze. "Yes, thank you very much indeed, Miss Wheeler, but Miss von Bismarck will not be able to join you this evening. She has been invited to sit at the captain's table for dinner. An invitation which understandably takes precedence over yours."

Meike resorted to humor to diffuse the growing tension. "I'm afraid the captain is quite enamored of me."

"Who isn't?" Despite her smile, Helen's eyes were deadly serious. They darted from Meike's face to Oskar's as if searching for something. "Tell you what," she said as if she had found what she sought. "If you can't join me for dinner, I think I'll join you. Save me a seat at the captain's table and I'll see you tonight."

Oskar gave Meike's arm another subtle squeeze, but she chose to ignore the warning.

"I look forward to it."

❖

Helen stared in the mirror above the bathroom sink as she knotted her bow tie to make sure both sides of the tie were coming out even. She wasn't especially vain about her appearance, but tonight she wanted to look good. Her assignment was to capture Meike's attention and she meant to do just that.

The outfit she had chosen to wear might garner her more attention than she wanted, but it was a price she was willing to pay. Meike liked seeing her in suits, and she was determined to give her what she wanted. And, perhaps, she'd get what she desired in return.

She erased visions of a naked Meike from her mind and returned her attention to the task at hand. The thought of Meike working with the Nazis was ridiculous, but if Uncle Sam wanted to pay her to prove what she already knew, so be it. She just had to remember to keep her heart out of the equation. She was supposed to make Meike fall in love with her, not the other way around. This time, like all the other times, she would be the one walking away, not the one left behind.

Swifty entered the room without knocking, then paused with his hand on the latch. "I know the dress code says black tie, kid, but I doubt this is what they meant."

Helen affixed tennis racquet-shaped cufflinks to the sleeves of her pressed white shirt. "Too much?"

"Not if you're trying to look like Marlene Dietrich in *Morocco*. In that case, you look perfect. Dietrich looked more comfortable kissing a woman in that picture than Gary Cooper did."

Helen buttoned her double-breasted tuxedo jacket and ran a hand over her slicked-back hair. "I've never had any problems in that department."

Swifty folded his arms across his chest as he leaned in the doorway. "I know. I've seen you in action. But if you insist on wearing those duds, I might be seeing you in handcuffs instead. This isn't Hollywood, kid. And it sure as hell isn't Harlem or wherever you picked up those two broads I saw you with at the Ritz-Carlton the morning that fed came to see you."

Helen swallowed the bitter aftertaste of her meeting with Agent Paul Lanier. She had given Swifty the bare bones of her meeting with Lanier, but she hadn't filled in all the details. If she told Swifty everything she had been asked to do, she would feel like an even bigger crumb for agreeing to do it.

She told herself she was doing what was best for her country, but in reality she knew she was only trying to save her own hide. Unconventional though it might be, tonight's outfit could be explained away with a wink and a smile or a fanciful lie. Lanier's pictures, however, left no room for doubt. If they fell into the wrong hands, her career would be over and her life would never be the same.

When her parents had caught her kissing her female friend from two doors down, her father had tried to beat the predilection out of her and her mother had tried to pray it away. Neither method had worked, so they had chosen to give up on her instead. But Helen had refused to give up on herself. One day, she had vowed, she would have everything she had ever wanted. Everything her parents said she didn't deserve to have. That day was almost here.

She had worked too hard for too long for her dreams to go up in smoke now that she was on the verge of making them come true, but she had to be true to herself. She was walking a fine line—and the line was getting narrower each day.

"We're hundreds of miles from shore, Swifty. What's the captain going to do when he sees me dressed like this, turn the boat around so he can hand me over to the boys in Gotham's vice squad? If I don't make it to Adelaide on time, he'll be hearing from the USLTA, followed pretty quickly by my lawyer."

"You don't have a lawyer."

"I don't need one when I have you."

Swifty rubbed the heel of his hand across his stubbled chin. His beard was so thick he usually developed five o'clock shadow well before noon, but his head was as smooth as Daddy Warbucks's.

"I'm glad I'm bald. If I had any hair left, you would have turned it gray by now. On second thought, you're probably the reason it all fell out in the first place."

"And you love me for it."

"I love you like you were my own daughter. That's why I wish you'd told our favorite fed to stick his offer where the sun don't shine. You're a tennis player, kid, not a spy. You're not cut out for what he wants you to do."

"You worry too much, Swifty." Helen patted his cheek to assuage the concern she heard in his voice. "I'll be fine."

"As long as you get the results Lanier wants. What happens if you don't come up with anything? Will he give you a pat on the back and say, 'Nice effort,' or does he plan to leave you holding the bag?"

Helen hadn't considered the possible consequences if her mission didn't go as planned. Would she end up in the slammer, her career brought to a premature end and her reputation ruined by a morals charge? She would face those obstacles when the time came. At the moment, the only questions she wanted answered concerned the big galoot she'd seen Meike with on deck a few hours earlier. Who was he and why was he plastered to Meike's side?

Helen had never seen a Nazi in person, but she was pretty sure Oskar Henkel was one. He looked just like the brainwashed, uniformed hordes she'd seen heiling Hitler on all the newsreels. Which made her wonder why one of the *Führer's* toadies was acting as Meike's chaperone. Had Meike, as Lanier suspected, become one of them or were they keeping her on a short leash until she did? Either way, it didn't look good.

"Are you sure about this?" Swifty asked as they made their way to the dining room.

Helen didn't know if he meant spying on Meike or wearing a tuxedo in public, but it didn't matter because she had already made up her mind about both. "I'm positive."

She heard the sounds as soon as she and Swifty walked into the dining room. Gasps of recognition followed by murmurs of disapproval. She had grown immune to the former. The latter still affected her much more than she wished they would. She told people she didn't care what the press wrote about her tirades on the court or her antics off it. In truth, she took everything that was said about her to heart. On the outside, she was an internationally famous tennis star. On the inside, she was still just a girl from Cannery Row.

The women at the dining tables were dripping in jewels, their shoulders protected from the chill by luxurious fur stoles. The men were just as polished, their gold and sterling silver accessories shining even brighter than the cut crystal chandeliers overhead. Helen might not have been born into this world, but she was here now and she was willing to do whatever it took to stay there. Even if it meant betraying a friend.

"The porters must have made a mix-up with the luggage," she joked after a high society matron looked at her and rolled her eyes. "Right now, some unlucky fella is trying to figure out how to squeeze himself into a size eight evening gown."

"Nice move, kid," Swifty said under his breath. "Always leave them laughing. It works every time."

"Usually," Helen said, remembering how her fondness for cracking jokes had often clashed with Meike's dour demeanor. Making Meike laugh for the first time had been an accomplishment even greater than winning a Grand Slam title. And making her come remained a feat beyond compare.

The men at the captain's table stood to greet her, though Oskar Henkel was noticeably slow to rise from his seat. "If the organizers of the Australian Championships plan to have a mixed singles competition," he said in German as she and Swifty claimed the last pair of available seats, "she would win every match six-love, six-love."

Meike frowned with disapproval, but her doubles partner, Liesel Becker, and their coach, former player Inge Kreuzer, tittered in amusement. Meike seemed to be about to speak, but Helen silenced her with a subtle shake of her head. She didn't need Meike's help. She could fight her own battles. She always had. She always would.

"You're not giving yourself enough credit, Oskar," she said as she spread her napkin in her lap. "I'm sure you would manage to win at least one game against me."

Helen's German was rusty, but based on Oskar's stunned expression, she had managed to get her point across.

Meike raised her linen napkin to her lips to hide her smile. Her whispered, *"Brava,"* held a hint of pride. It should have. She was the one who had given Helen German lessons in the first place. One of many things Meike had taught her over the years.

"Don Budge and Gene Mako are playing jazz albums on a portable phonograph in their room every night, and I have you lovely ladies sitting at my table." Captain Ruston Kelly took a sip of red wine as formally attired waiters brought out the first of six courses. "How did I manage to have so many stars from the tennis constellation on board my ship?"

"You're just lucky, I guess," Helen said.

"Since you have so many valuable commodities on board, make sure you steer clear of any icebergs."

Swifty's joke provoked a round of nervous laughter. Tales of the *Titanic*'s sinking had faded into history, but the disaster's effects still lingered twenty-five years later. Helen would keep an anxious eye on the water until the *Southern Star* pulled into port several weeks from now, and she felt certain many other passengers would be doing the same, but she doubted any of them wanted to talk about it over caviar and smoked oysters at the captain's table. She tried to lift the mood, which had quickly turned from lighthearted to leaden. "If you're sitting here next to me, Cap, who's doing the driving?"

"My second in command. I get all the acclaim," Captain Kelly whispered conspiratorially, "but Staff Captain Hardwick does most of the work."

"Is that how you felt when you and I played doubles together, Meike?" Helen asked.

"You were a more than capable partner," Meike said in heavily accented but perfect English. "I had to work hard to hold up my end of the partnership."

"Now she makes me carry the load," Liesel said.

Helen laughed politely because she knew what Liesel had said couldn't possibly be true. Meike could win a doubles match by herself if she wanted, but Liesel couldn't even win in singles without help.

Liesel was a good player but not a great one. She was solid and didn't make many mistakes. Playing her was like playing against a backboard. She got every ball back. She allowed her opponents to defeat themselves because she didn't have the offensive weapons to do it on her own. Her ability to do everything equally well made her an excellent doubles player, but it didn't do much for her singles game. She had no problems defeating the players ranked below her, but she struggled against the ones ranked above her. She might give the top seeds a scare if they were having an off day, but she wasn't a serious threat to pull off the upset. Off the court wasn't much different. She was pretty, but, unlike Meike, she wasn't a classic beauty. Then again, few were.

The first time Helen had played Meike, she had been so taken by the view from across the net, she had barely managed to win points let alone games. Despite the lopsided final result, she must have made a good impression because Meike had asked her to be her doubles partner at the next week's event. Unless representing her country, Helen hadn't played with anyone else for the next four years. She had thought they would be partners for the rest of their careers. Then, without warning, Meike had pulled the plug. Despite their excellent track record, Meike had pushed her away because she "needed some distance."

Helen had had trouble accepting the explanation then, and she wasn't buying it now. Now she needed to convince Meike it wasn't distance they needed but proximity. And tonight was the perfect time to start.

❖

After dinner, Meike took a stroll on the promenade deck to walk off a few of the courses from the lavish meal and to escape the thick cloud of cigar smoke that had begun to fill the dining room almost as soon as the dessert plates were cleared from the tables. She heard the band warming up in the showroom on the lido deck two floors above, but she didn't plan to partake in the evening's entertainment. Because tonight she didn't feel like dancing.

When Helen had announced she planned to become a professional player, Meike hadn't expected to see her again. Yet here she was. What were the odds they would book passage to Australia on the same ship? After not seeing each other for several months, they would be forced to see each other every day for the next several weeks. Even longer if they both reached the final in Adelaide. They had both ended the season playing so well Meike didn't expect anyone to get in their way. Except, perhaps, each other.

Just like old times.

Seeing Helen on deck this afternoon had left her feeling grateful for a friendly face. For the possibility of having someone to converse with freely and openly without the heavy burden of self-censorship. Seeing Helen tonight, however, looking so dapper in her tuxedo and coming up with such a clever rejoinder to Oskar's crass comment, had left her feeling shaken.

According to press speculation, she had stopped playing doubles with Helen because of their budding rivalry in singles. She didn't want to spend too much time with Helen, they wrote, because she didn't want Helen to pick up on the secrets of her game and use them to defeat her. She had never commented on the speculation because it was too dangerous for her to try to separate fact from fiction. In order to retain both her privacy and her freedom, she needed to be circumspect about her private life, not make it fodder for public consumption.

The reason she had ended such a successful partnership was a simple one. It was also deeply personal. She had stopped playing doubles with Helen because she found it increasingly difficult to control her attraction to her. They were together so often it was only natural for the warm feelings between them to deepen into something more meaningful, which made playing against each other a contest of will as well as skill. A contest Meike didn't think she could win. As a result, their personal relationship had suffered as well.

When she had looked across the net during their singles matches, she hadn't seen a nameless, faceless opponent trying to prevent her from accomplishing the goals she had set for herself when she first took up the sport. What she saw was the face of a woman she had started to love. In the end, she had been forced to choose between personal happiness and professional success. Sometimes, she wondered if she had made the wrong choice. But in tennis, the only place for love was on the scoreboard. And in Nazi Germany, love had no place at all. Which meant Helen could never be part of her life again.

"Careful of the ice, Miss von Bismarck," Oskar said as he followed a short distance behind her. "We wouldn't want you to fall overboard."

Snow had been falling steadily all day, covering everything in a blanket of white. Dozens of the ship's workers toiled diligently to keep the walkway clear and to knock ice off the railings and various metal surfaces, but several slippery patches remained.

Meike trailed a gloved hand along the railing, ready to grab hold in case she lost her balance. Even though she didn't consider Oskar's words a threat, she reflexively tightened her grip. Life would be much easier for him if she were to meet with an unfortunate accident. He could return to Berlin and protect someone who agreed with his ideals, not stand watch over someone who didn't.

"No," she said. "We wouldn't want that."

He glanced at the steadily darkening sky. "Miss Becker has already turned in for the evening. Perhaps it is time you did the same. It has been a long day. You need to get plenty of rest if you want to play your best tennis in Australia."

Meike turned to face him. Startled by the move, Oskar pulled up short. "I didn't know you were a fan, Oskar. I thought you would prefer to see me lose rather than win."

The corners of his mouth lifted in a smile strangely devoid of mirth.

"A victory for you is a victory for the Fatherland. I celebrate your accomplishments, Miss von Bismarck, even though I vehemently disagree with your lifestyle and your choice of…friends." Meike's face must have betrayed her shock because Oskar's smile grew even more malicious. "Yes, I know about your predilections. I have read your file. With some disgust, I might add."

Meike wanted to defend herself, but she knew there was nothing she could say to change his mind, no matter how eloquent her argument.

"I know how much the American meant to you. I know she was much more than your doubles partner. Have you discussed our situation with her?"

"I haven't discussed our 'situation,' as you describe it, with anyone. Who you are and why you're here is of no concern to anyone but me."

She didn't want to involve anyone else in her troubles. Not Friedrich, not her family, and especially not Helen.

"Good. For Miss Wheeler's sake, I mean. Even if you did tell her about me, your situation would remain unchanged. If the cowardly Americans won't do anything to save the lives of thousands of Jews, do you honestly think they would lift a finger to save yours? You are two things politicians hate the most: an aristocrat and a homosexual. Aristocracy has its place in the new Germany, but homosexuality must be eradicated at all costs."

Meike felt renewed fear. Not only for herself but the friends she had left behind. Friends like Friedrich, for whom freedom came at a price much steeper than the one that had been placed on their heads.

"You are too valuable to be punished at the present, but if your value were to diminish…"

Even though Oskar didn't finish his sentence, Meike heard the words he didn't say. The words the Austrian had made explicitly clear the last time she had been taken to Nazi headquarters to see him. She was safe as long as she continued to win tennis tournaments and garner positive press attention for Germany. But if she began to lose more matches than she won—perhaps even if she lost only one, provided the tournament was important enough—she would spend the rest of her life in a concentration camp.

Her goals for the upcoming tennis season needed to change. Next year was no longer about trying to secure her place in history. It was about trying to stay alive.

CHAPTER THREE

December 1937
The Atlantic Ocean

Helen stood on the edge of the crowd as she watched Meike conduct a practice session with Liesel Becker under the watchful eyes of Inge Kreuzer and Oskar Henkel. Meike had kept to herself for the past several days, taking her meals in her room and only venturing out to practice for two hours a day on the indoor tennis court on the sports deck or to pace on the veranda outside her suite. Helen's sightings of her were just like this one. From afar.

"She's looking good," Swifty said after Meike whistled a forehand winner past Liesel's outstretched racquet.

"I know," Helen said, watching Meike's smooth calves flash beneath her long tennis skirt as she glided along the baseline.

Helen went on twice-daily walks around the promenade deck to stay in shape during the trip, but she had taken the court only twice this week. She had played one practice set against Don Budge and another against his doubles partner, Gene Mako.

Returning Don's powerful serves was a challenge for Helen. So was tracking down his fearsome forehand. But she usually managed to direct enough balls to his slightly more vulnerable backhand wing to make the score relatively respectable. Despite the losses, competing against the best male player in the world did wonders for her game.

As for Gene, he hit the ball with so much spin Helen never knew which way the ball would bounce when it landed. He played table tennis the same way. Helen felt like an abject beginner when she played against him, but his constant stream of jokes made the embarrassment worthwhile—and eased the pressure of competing at the highest level. Being around Gene reminded her that, despite the high stakes, tennis was just a game. Something to be enjoyed, not fretted over.

Seeing a man and a woman play singles against each other must have been a rarity for the gathered crowd, but for Helen it was nothing unusual. She, Don, and Gene were all native Californians and had known each other for years. Whenever they played the same events, they always made time to get together to hit a few balls and listen to the jazz albums Don never went anywhere without. San Francisco native Alice Marble sometimes joined them, but not often. Alice's coach, Eleanor "Teach" Tennant, kept her on such a short leash, all Alice was allowed to do was train, practice, and play. Then again, after losing a year of her career to illness and injury, Alice was lucky to be alive, let alone playing tennis at an elite level once more.

Helen wished Alice, home in Los Angeles nursing an ankle injury, had been healthy enough to compete in Australia. Alice had worked her way back up the rankings and had positioned herself one notch below her in both the national and world standings. Helen wanted a chance to prove herself against Alice in the crucible of a major. And she wanted a chance to prove her critics wrong.

Critics said she had become America's top female amateur player due to Alice's absence in parts of 1934 and 1935, not because she had made the necessary improvements in her game.

Going up against Alice would have to wait, however. For the time being, she had to "settle" for the chance to beat Meike instead, a feat she—or anyone else—had not accomplished in far too long. It had been years since Meike had tasted defeat. And once they got to Adelaide, Helen meant to give her a good, healthy dose.

She nodded appreciatively after Meike drew Liesel wide with an American twist serve and won the point with a crisp volley off Liesel's weak return. Meike didn't serve and volley often, but her net game was just as efficient as her baseline game. If she decided to play more aggressively, she would be even harder to defeat. Harder but not impossible. When she was serving well, Helen was pretty tough to beat, too.

Swifty moved his unlit cigar from one side of his mouth to the other. "Do you think you can beat her?"

"We'll see when we get to Adelaide."

"Why not now? You don't want to let a perfectly good court go to waste, do you?"

Helen knew she needed to sharpen her skills before the Australian Championships, but the tournament was nearly a month away. It was too soon to concentrate on serious tennis. It was too soon to concentrate on anything except her assignment: getting closer to Meike.

"I would love to see what she's been working on during the offseason, but I doubt she'd be foolish enough to tip her hand so soon. The next time I'm across the net from her, I want it to be for real."

"I've got money riding on you, kid."

"Yours or someone else's?"

Swifty continued to chomp on his sodden cigar. "You heard about my good night at the poker table, did you?"

"How much dough did you fleece out of your playing partners?"

Swifty pulled up his sleeve so she could take a gander at the shiny new watch that had belonged to someone else less than twenty-four hours ago. "Enough to pad my pockets a little and whet the losers' appetites for an opportunity to win back their stash. I can't clean them out too soon. There's still too much open water between me and land if I need to make a quick getaway."

"You're not stacking the deck again, are you?"

"I prefer to call it playing the percentages. Isn't that what you do when you play an opponent who's better than you?"

Helen stiffened. When it came to winning and losing, she didn't like coming in second. No matter what the world rankings said, she knew she was just as good a player as Meike if not better. "There's no one who's better than I am."

"Oh, yeah? Prove it."

"When the Australian Championships start, I intend to do just that."

Even with Meike in the field, she was going to win in Adelaide. She could feel it in her bones. The grass courts were slick and fast. Perfect for her aggressive game. The slow red clay at Roland Garros better suited Meike's baseline game, so Helen was prepared to concede her the French Championships, though not without a fight. That left Wimbledon and the US Championships, both played on grass.

If she played her game and didn't let Meike get under her skin, Helen could win three majors next season and, if she racked up enough titles at smaller tournaments, she had an outside chance of finishing the year ranked number one. Next year could be her year. Then she could sign the contract Lanier had strong-armed her into tearing up. A contract that could have netted her one hundred thousand dollars instead of the fraction Uncle Sam had agreed to pay.

She forced herself to put thoughts of the future aside, however, and concentrate on the present. She had work to do. If she had her way, tonight was the night she finally began to draw some information out of Meike. Information that might put both their lives at risk.

What would the Nazis do to Meike if they thought she was compromised? What would they do to her if they discovered she was trying to find out what they were up to? There was only one thing she could do to prevent either scenario from occurring: not get caught.

"Do you have an extra set of cards, Swifty?" she asked as she watched Meike and Liesel shake hands to conclude their practice session.

"Sure, kid. Why do you want to know?"

"Tonight, I want to play a game of my own."

❖

Meike pushed the remnants of her dinner around her plate. She knew she needed to eat in order to maintain her strength, but her appetite had deserted her the instant Oskar made his pronouncement the week before.

You are too valuable to be punished at the present, but if your value were to diminish…

Meike placed the domed cover over her nearly full plate and held her head in her hands. Had the time come for her to seek political asylum? Should she reach out to the governments of Switzerland, France, or the United States to see if they would take her in? No. If what Oskar said was true, no government officials would be willing to intercede on her behalf. For better or worse, she was in charge of her own fate. If she wanted to stay alive—if she wanted to keep her loved ones safe, she had to keep winning.

On the court, she maintained a semblance of control. Off it, she had never felt more helpless or lost. The Australian Championships couldn't begin quickly enough. She needed to focus her energy on something tangible before she became completely overwhelmed. She needed a chance to prove her worth. Then, perhaps, she could make demands instead of conceding to them.

Too many thoughts were running through her head. A knock on her stateroom door provided a temporary and much-needed distraction. Instead of the room service waiter come to collect her tray, she opened the door to find Helen standing in the hall, a devilish grin on her face and a pack of playing cards in her hand.

"Do you feel lucky?" Helen asked in a sultry growl.

Meike didn't know how to respond. Was Helen asking her to rekindle their former relationship or embark on something new? Both options were tempting, though equally doomed to fail. Looking at the pack of cards, she said, "That depends on the game being played."

Helen's gray-green eyes twinkled. "What if I said the game was strip poker?"

Meike felt a flash of desire she tried and failed to extinguish. She and Helen had always been rivals on court. In bed, however, they had never been anything but allies, united in their pursuit of pleasure. "Then I suppose I would feel very lucky indeed."

"May I come in?"

Helen's voice dropped another octave, falling into a range that made the nascent flame stirring inside Meike burn a little brighter. She knew she should say no. She didn't need another complication in her already too-complicated life. And no matter what the outcome, there was no way she could win the game Helen was proposing. One night of passion would only provoke even more memories of the past. But thanks to her uncertain future, anything more than one night was an impossible dream.

Putting past, present, and future aside, she opened the door wider and said, "Yes, please do."

❖

Helen examined the cards in her hand and considered her options. Meike had proven to be even more adept at five-card draw than she was at tennis.

They had started the evening wearing the same amount of clothing—Meike in an evening gown complete with the requisite accessories and Helen in a suit and tie. Two games later, Meike was still nearly fully dressed and Helen had been reduced to her boxer shorts, bra, A-line undershirt, and dress socks. The rest of her clothes, including her prized cufflinks, were piled on Meike's side of the table. The way Helen's cards looked, the rest of her outfit would be joining the pile soon.

Her hand was crap. Five cards and not a single pair. She had an outside shot at a straight if she traded in three of her cards and pulled the right ones off the deck, but she didn't like the odds. So she decided to do what she did best: bluff.

"How many cards would you like?" she asked, resting her fingers on the brightly colored deck.

Meike pressed a finger against her pursed lips, then tossed two cards on the table facedown and asked for two more.

Helen dealt Meike the requested cards but didn't bother to take another look at her own hand. "Dealer stands pat." She fought to suppress a smile when Meike raised a questioning eyebrow. "What's your opening bid?" she asked, idly stroking one of the satin evening gloves she had won in the first hand before Meike nearly cleaned her out in the second.

Meike's brow furrowed as if she was considering where to direct her serve during the crucial stages of a championship match. "I'll bet…my earrings and necklace."

Helen regarded the cultured pearl necklace circling Meike's throat. Meike's pulse beat slowly and steadily but seemed to quicken the longer Helen's eyes lingered on the intoxicating spot where Meike's neck met her shoulder. She could stare at that spot all day. Preferably all night.

She slowly shifted her gaze from the pearl necklace to the glittering diamond drop earrings dangling from Meike's earlobes. She wouldn't wear the jewelry if she won it—both the necklace and the earrings were much too fancy for her taste—but perhaps she could keep the pairing as a souvenir or, more likely, present them as a gift to her next one-night stand.

"I will bet you my socks and undershirt and raise you my bra."

The pulse at the base of Meike's throat quickened even more. When she spoke, her voice was husky with desire. "Though I would enjoy the resulting view if I were fortunate enough to win this hand, I doubt your bet would be considered a fair trade, even on the black market."

Helen had two choices: she could attempt to seduce Meike or she could go after the information Lanier had asked her to seek. She made her choice quickly so she wouldn't have time to second-guess herself.

"Are you familiar with how the black market works? You must be, considering how many people are willing to barter everything they own in exchange for a one-way ticket out of Germany."

Meike's eyes narrowed. She parted her lips as if to respond, then quickly clamped them shut. "I'm sure such things occur," she said after a lengthy pause, "but no one has approached me looking to make any deals."

"Would you be willing to listen if they did? Or are you allowing Oskar Henkel to speak for you now? Who is he to you, anyway? At dinner my first night on board, I thought he had a soft spot for Liesel. Whenever I see him, though, he's glued to your side instead of hers. What do you think he'd do if he knew you and I were together right now? Would he be jealous or vengeful?"

Helen remembered how Meike had cowed in Oskar's presence the day she had encountered them on deck. She didn't like seeing Meike so docile. So…afraid. She had assumed Oskar had been assigned by the German Tennis Association to keep its biggest star safe, but perhaps he was here to make sure she followed orders. Hitler's orders.

Meike lifted her steel blue eyes from her cards and focused them on Helen's face. "Is there a reason you are asking me such questions?" she asked with more than a hint of challenge in her voice.

Because my government wants me to.

"Because perhaps I'm the jealous one."

"Oskar and I aren't together, Helen." Meike lowered her eyes as well as her voice. "Neither, I must remind you, are we."

"Believe me, you don't have to remind me. How could I possibly forget?" Helen reached for Meike's hand, but Meike pulled away before Helen could receive the contact she sought. "Why did you leave me?"

Meike's eyes shuttered, preventing Helen from peering into her soul. "Do you want me to tell you the truth, or would you prefer me to spare your feelings?"

Helen leaned back in her chair. "I want to know. Why did you break up with me when we were having such a good time?"

Meike smiled sadly. "We were opposites, Helen. We still are. I take everything too seriously and you don't take anything seriously enough. You drift through life, floating aimlessly from one experience to another. You have no anchor. No stability. I can't live like that. I need someone I can depend on when times are tough, not someone who trivializes the issue by offering to take me dancing or tell a funny joke."

Helen wanted to say something in her defense, but she remained silent because she knew what Meike had said was true. "Always leave them laughing" was not only Swifty's favorite motto but hers as well. Sometimes, she had to laugh to keep from crying, though that wasn't something she was willing to admit. Who would care, anyway?

"There's more to life than having fun, Helen."

"And there's more to life than tennis, Meike. There are more important things than winning and being number one. Being second best has its spoils, too. If you weren't so determined to make history, you'd make time to enjoy the present. Relax a little. Have some fun. Like we used to."

Meike looked almost nostalgic, but only for a moment. "Each of us has a chance to make a mark in history. I don't want to waste my opportunity. I want to leave a legacy behind. When my career's over, I want to be able to say I didn't waste an ounce of my talent."

"Is that what you think I'm doing?" Helen was used to press and fans questioning her commitment to her sport. They saw her going out at night, staying up too late, and occasionally drinking too much and wondered how much she really wanted to win. But Meike, of all people, knew how hard she worked. How hard she trained. How much she wanted to win. Meike knew her. Didn't she?

Meike eyed the half-empty bottle of Dom Perignon on Helen's side of the table. Helen smiled and poured herself another glass.

"Wasting talent is one thing. Wasting good champagne is another." The corners of Meike's lips curled upward, easing the tension that had threatened to take the fun out of their game. "I'm glad to see you smile. If I have my way, you're going to be doing a lot of that this year."

"Because?"

"I have two goals for the season: to beat you at least once and to get you to lighten up."

"How do you expect to accomplish your goals?"

Helen sipped her champagne. "I haven't figured that part out yet."

"I wish you luck on both counts," Meike said, obviously trying not to smile, "but did you come to my room tonight to talk about tennis or play cards?"

Helen followed Meike's lead. The night was young and her assignment had barely begun. She didn't want to push Meike too far too soon. If she did, she could lose her for good. "Your move," she said, expecting Meike to fold.

Meike glanced at her cards and rearranged them as if putting them in order. Either she had the superior hand or she was even better at bluffing than Helen was. "I'm, how do you say, all in."

"Wait." Helen looked down at her skimpy outfit before looking over at Meike's nearly intact one. "I think that's my line."

Meike leaned forward, obviously waiting for Helen to match her bet or concede defeat. "So I win?"

Even when she knew she was beaten, Helen was no quitter. "Not so fast. I call." She gathered her cards and prepared to reveal them. "Same time?" Meike nodded and they laid their cards on the table. Helen laughed long and loud when she realized that, like her, Meike had a handful of nothing. Thanks to her ten of clubs, Helen held high card. "My crap hand wasn't so crappy after all. Looks like I win this round."

"And I lose."

"Don't worry." Helen sat up straight to get a better view of the upcoming show. "I promise to make losing worth your while."

With a resigned sigh, Meike placed her earrings and necklace on the table. Then she stood and rested her foot in her chair. After she reached under her dress, she unsnapped her garter, slowly peeled off one of her silk stockings, and tossed it in Helen's direction. Helen closed her eyes as she passed the delicate fabric under her nose and inhaled the heady scent of Meike's perfume, but she quickly opened them when she heard Meike switch legs and begin to remove her other stocking.

Helen draped Meike's stockings around her neck and clenched her hands into fists to keep from reaching inside her boxer shorts to relieve the growing tension in her groin. How could one woman possibly be so beautiful? Her breath caught as she watched Meike slowly unveil herself. She wanted to see more—much more—but she rose from her seat before Meike could give her what she wanted.

"*Nein*," she said with a firm shake of her head. She grazed her fingertips over Meike's skin as she slipped the thin spaghetti strap of Meike's evening gown back onto her shapely shoulder. "Not tonight."

Meike's eyes asked the question her slightly parted lips didn't form. *Why?*

"When you reveal yourself to me again," Helen said, fighting to keep her voice steady, "I want it to be of your own free will rather than obligation. I want you to be with me because you want to, not because you lost a bet."

Meike's pupils dilated, indicating she might be amenable to a kiss and, perhaps, much more. Unlike at the card table, Helen decided not to press her luck. Instead, she indicated the twin piles of discarded clothing. "Trade you?"

Meike smiled, something Helen wished she would do a lot more of. "Only if you promise to grant me a rematch one day soon."

Helen was pleased to see her gambit tonight had worked. She had Meike's attention. The next step was gaining her interest. But based on Meike's reaction to her touch, she already had that, too. One thing was for sure. Meike definitely had hers. "Before Adelaide or after?" she asked as she got dressed.

"After."

"Naturally."

Meike obviously didn't want anything to distract her from her preparations for the Australian Championships. In that respect, tonight was definitely the exception to the rule.

Distraction or not, Helen wasn't going to go away. She was filled with questions, and only Meike could provide the answers. Questions about Meike's role in Hitler's plans for Germany.

Questions about Oskar Henkel's dubious presence in her life. And, most importantly, questions about what role—if any—she might have in Meike's future now that they were finally taking steps to put the past to rest.

Helen formed her tie into a Windsor knot, shrugged on her suit jacket, and bade Meike good night. Lanier was expecting her to send him a detailed report when she arrived in Adelaide, but she didn't have anything to give him. Despite her win at the poker table, she felt like the evening had ended in a draw.

But the stakes were about to get much higher. Because the next time she and Meike met, there would be a trophy on the line.

CHAPTER FOUR

January 1938
Adelaide, Australia

At the Australian Championships, nearly half the competitors in the ninety-six player fields in both the men's and women's draws were citizens of the host country. As she played Aussie after Aussie during the tournament's early rounds, Meike encountered raucous crowds but met with little resistance from her opponents. She won her first match in twelve minutes and her second in fifteen. Not counting her doubles matches, which also passed in practically no time at all, she reached the singles semifinals having spent a total of less than an hour on the court.

As a rule, continuous play made tennis matches go by quickly on any surface—most five-set matches were completed in about an hour, and any match that lasted more than two hours was considered an epic test of endurance—but grass courts shortened points, speeding up the pace even more.

Meike thought the courts at Wimbledon were quick. But that was before she set foot on the lightning-fast courts in Adelaide, where most points didn't last more than three strokes and the majority of games were contested in under a minute.

Her concern about wilting in the heat appeared to have been for naught. After she crushed former champ Joan Hartigan in the semifinals, she felt like she had put herself in the perfect position to win her first singles title in Adelaide. Doubles, too, if she and Liesel continued to advance. She was playing well and she had plenty of energy left, despite the oppressive conditions. Her only concern at this point—other than avoiding injury in the doubles semifinal—was finding a way to derail the freight train that was Helen Wheeler.

Helen had struggled in her opening match, forced to go three sets to defeat fellow American Dorothy Cheney. Once she got past that hurdle 10-12, 8-6, 6-4, she had looked unbeatable. Every part of her game was working—her volleys, her groundstrokes, and especially her serve. In fact, she was serving so well, she had struck more aces than some of the competitors in the men's field, a tally she added to when she whitewashed last year's runner-up Emily Hood Westacott in the semifinals to set up a match against Meike for the singles championship.

"Helen is playing brutally efficient tennis," a reporter said as Meike and Liesel made their way to the court to play their doubles semifinal against two-time defending champions Thelma Coyne Long and Nancy Wynne Bolton. "How do you plan to defeat her?"

Meike planned to play the singles final with a mixture of aggression and patience, but she didn't want to give away her strategy in case Helen got wind of it in time to form a successful counterattack.

Helen was playing better tennis than Meike had ever seen her play and she had two important intangibles in her favor: she was more familiar with the court and, thanks to winning three consecutive titles, she was a huge favorite with the fans. The Australians had practically adopted her as one of their own. Playing her in the final would be like going up against yet another Aussie.

The oddsmakers said Meike was the slight favorite in the final, but she felt like the underdog. Beating Helen would be a difficult task. Meike didn't want to spot her any unnecessary advantages.

She carefully considered the reporter's question, then smiled in his general direction and said, "My plan to defeat Helen? Winning the final point."

❖

"It's a scorcher out here, kid." Swifty fanned his sweaty face with his fedora as he and Helen climbed into the backseat of a taxi to make the short ride from their hotel to the tennis stadium. "The thermometer in the window of that barber shop over there reads thirty-eight degrees Celsius. I couldn't tell you how to translate Celsius into Fahrenheit if you paid me, but I don't need to know the exact temperature to know that spells H-O-T hot. You and Meike will be up against it today. I heard fans are already fainting in their seats and play hasn't even started yet."

Helen placed a wet cabbage leaf in the lining of her cap to combat the heat, a trick Alice Marble had picked up from the farm workers she had come across in her youth. Helen used to make fun of her old friend's peculiar habit—until she tried it for herself and experienced the amazing results.

The cab's leather seats burned the backs of her flannel shorts-covered legs. She wished she had waited until she got to the locker room to don her tennis attire, but it was too late to change her mind now.

"Are you trying to make me feel better about my prospects or worse?"

"I'm just letting you know what you're in for, that's all. I still believe in you, kid. Before the tournament started, I bet on you to win the triple."

Helen had opted to play singles, doubles, and mixed doubles in Adelaide, and she had managed to make the finals of all three events. After she and Meike squared off in singles, they would face each other again in doubles. At the end of her busy day—if she was still standing by then—she and Don Budge would contest the mixed doubles final against Australians John Bromwich and Margaret Wilson.

Thanks to Swifty's comment, Helen felt the pressure to win ratchet up even higher. On the way to Adelaide, he had said he loved her like a daughter. She thought his feelings for her were genuine, but tennis, like any other major sport, was a business. If he found another player he thought he could take to the pinnacle instead of the penultimate spot, she had no doubt he would turn his back on her before the ink dried on the new kid's contract. Where would that leave her? Where she'd been all her life: on the outside looking in.

She had to win today. Not only to narrow the gap between herself and Meike but to widen the one between herself and the players nipping at her heels.

"I'll try not to let you down, Swifty."

He placed a reassuring hand on her knee. When he spoke, his voice was as gentle as his touch. "I was kidding about the bet, kid. I wouldn't dream of putting that much extra weight on your shoulders. Well, I might," he added with a wink, "but I'd be smart enough not to tell you about it until the matches were over."

The cabbie pulled to a stop outside the stadium, put the car in Park, and jumped out to open the door. Swifty held up a hand to ask for a few minutes alone. The cabbie nodded and backed away, mingling with a few members of the steadily growing crowd while he waited for his fare.

"I know the title you really want, kid, and it isn't doubles or mixed. Now go out there and get it."

The tension in Helen's shoulders loosened and the butterflies in her stomach stopped flapping their wings. "Yes, sir."

She screwed her cap on tight, prepared to show Meike she was the three-time defending champion for a reason. Prepared to put an end to Meike's vaunted winning streak once and for all. She climbed out of the car to a deafening round of applause.

"Last year might have been her year," she said to herself as she waved to the cheering fans, "but this year's going to be mine."

❖

Meike and Helen stood in the tunnel leading to the court, matching bouquets of flowers in their arms. Despite her calm exterior, Meike was a bundle of nerves before every final, especially a major. Helen, on the other hand, looked as cool as the proverbial cucumber. "Good luck today."

Helen looked at Meike's outstretched hand for a long moment before she finally reached to grasp it. "The same to you. Today, you're going to need it."

Helen spoke with a steely determination. Meike hoped Helen's words wouldn't prove prophetic. If the card game she and Helen had played on the *Southern Star* was any indication, luck was most assuredly not on her side.

Adrenaline coursed through her body as she remembered the look in Helen's eyes and on her face while she attempted to pay the bet she had lost. She could still feel Helen's fingers grazing over her skin, searing her flesh as Helen adjusted the strap of her gown and said in a voice husky with desire, "When you reveal yourself to me again, I want it to be of your own free will rather than obligation. I want you to be with me because you want to, not because you lost a bet."

When she ended her relationship with Helen, she had thought she would never feel Helen's touch again. Now she didn't know if she would be able to live without it.

"Miss von Bismarck?"

The voice of chair umpire Simon Cahill pulled Meike out of her reverie. She realized with a start Simon and Helen were staring at her. "Yes?" she asked, wondering how long they had been waiting for her to respond to a question that had gone unheard.

"Shall we take the court?"

Helen slowly unspooled a knowing smile. Had she been able to read Meike's thoughts? The twinkle in her eyes certainly said so. Meike looked away to hide her growing discomfort. "Yes, of course. I think the fans have been waiting long enough."

"If you're feeling the heat, Meike," Helen said under her breath, "I know a few ways to cool you off. How about we start with a bucket of ice and a bottle of champagne? If handled properly, both could prove equally intoxicating."

With Helen around, Meike had a hard enough time keeping her wits about her. She didn't need to add alcohol and the lure of sex to the equation. "Thank you for your kind offer," she said with what she hoped was a polite smile, "but I am sure I will manage just fine."

Helen shrugged as if to say, "Your loss."

Meike felt it already.

She hoped missing out on an opportunity to spend time with Helen was the only loss she would experience today, but once the match that the press and fans alike had been anticipating for weeks finally began, she was forced to put thoughts of victory aside and settle for simply trying to find a way to make the match competitive.

The first set was over before late-arriving fans could settle into their seats. Meike couldn't remember the last time she had been so thoroughly outplayed. Unable to equal Helen's power or passion, she was buried under a barrage of aces, smashes, and sizzling groundstrokes as she lost the set 6-0.

She stared in disbelief as the numbers were affixed to the hand-operated scoreboard. In her entire career, she had never lost a set without winning a game. Even as a rank beginner pitted against far more experienced opponents, she had managed to string enough points together to capture at least one game. Now, many years later, she was allegedly the best player in the sport. And she'd just been blanked in the first set of a tournament she couldn't afford to lose.

Helen was right when she had said there was more to life than tennis. Unfortunately, the sentiment didn't apply to her. She longed for the days when winning and losing didn't feel like a matter of life and death. But those days were over. Perhaps for good.

As she prepared to serve to begin the second set, she was tasked with the unfamiliar challenge of having to come from behind—and cast in the unexpected role of underdog. For the past three years, this had been Helen's court. And the way she was playing today, she obviously didn't want her to reign to end.

The crowd's rhythmic applause was meant to lift Meike's spirits, but it only made her feel more embarrassed about her performance. Or lack thereof. For the first time in years, her fear of losing exceeded her will to win. If she didn't reverse course soon, the match, her winning streak—and, perhaps, her life— could be over in a matter of minutes.

As she stood on the baseline and waited for the crowd to grow quiet so play could resume, she chanced a peek into the stands. Oskar was sitting between Inge and Liesel. His arms were folded across his chest and, despite the score—or perhaps because of it—he looked like the match was going exactly the way he wanted it to. The Austrian and the rest of the Reich might be unhappy about the result if the second set followed the same pattern as the first. Oskar, however, could barely contain his delight.

The smug look on Oskar's face gave Meike the inspiration she needed to keep fighting. To remain patient. To wait for Helen's level of play to drop just enough to give her a chance to get back into the match. No matter how much energy she needed to expend or how long the task would take, she was going to turn Oskar's smirk into a frown. She was going to win.

"Thank you."

She accepted a ball from the ball boy and bounced it once, twice, three times. She hadn't been able to find a rhythm on her serve all day, but now was as good a time as any to start.

She took a deep breath, slowly released it, and tossed the ball into the air. Her racquet rose to strike the fuzzy, grass-stained orb just before it reached the apex of its flight. In the fraction of a second before her racquet made contact with the ball, Meike saw Helen out of the corner of her eye. Helen took a step to her forehand side, obviously expecting Meike to draw her out wide with an American twist serve. Indeed, that was what Meike had initially planned to do. Helen's shift in position indicated she knew Meike's playing patterns almost as well as Meike did. The action confirmed Meike's decision to end their doubles partnership. Helen knew her game—knew *her*—too well.

Helen would always have a place in her heart. In her mind, however, there was room for only one.

Instead of giving Helen what she expected, it was time to give her what she didn't. She decided to abandon her baseline tactics and take the net every time she had a chance to move forward. She decided to play like Helen.

She served an ace down the middle to open the game, then won the game at love by playing serve-and-volley on each point.

She played chip and charge when it was Helen's turn to serve, slicing her returns of the powerful deliveries to keep the ball low, then rushing to the net. Helen missed her first attempted passing shot. Then another. And another.

Meike broke her at love, consolidated the break to go up 3-0, and broke again to extend her lead even more.

Even though Helen was still winning the match, Meike could feel her starting to panic. Little by little, Helen's confidence began to waver. Her game began to unravel, followed soon after by her control over her emotions.

The calm, cool, almost cocky persona Helen had displayed before the match gradually disappeared. In its place came Hell on Wheels, the tantrum-throwing character fans loved to hate.

Helen hurled her racquet halfway across the court after Meike closed out the second set 6-0. The reporters in press row ate it up as they gleefully wrote updates to their still-developing stories, but the crowd whistled its disapproval.

Meike stepped away from the baseline and raised a finger to her lips, but her efforts to calm the riled-up crowd were for naught.

"Quiet, please," Simon Cahill said, making his own attempt to silence the din. "The players are ready."

The crowd protested a few minutes more, then the boos and whistles gradually began to subside. Despite the change in momentum in the second set, Meike expected Helen to fight as hard as she could in the third to retain her title—and regain her dignity.

She looked into Helen's eyes as she stood on the baseline and prepared to play the first point of the deciding set. What she saw simultaneously comforted and saddened her: Helen didn't think she could win.

❖

Helen's heart sank as she watched Meike's passing shot blow by her and land on the baseline. Meike's latest in a long string of winners had just won her the Australian Championships.

Meike thrust her arms in the air and skipped to the net as the chair umpire called out the final score.

"Game, set, match, Miss von Bismarck. Miss von Bismarck wins 0-6, 6-0, 6-2."

Simon Cahill's voice was nearly drowned out by the spectators' deafening applause. And the blazing sun overhead paled in comparison to Meike's dazzling smile. Helen could tell how much the win meant to Meike, but she was too disappointed by her humbling defeat to offer more than cursory congratulations as she and Meike shook hands at the net.

She unscrewed the stainless steel flask she had secreted in the shadows of the umpire's chair, took a sip of brandy for fortification, and put on a brave smile as she watched Meike being presented with the trophy she had hoped to raise for the fourth time. She forced herself to wait until she reached the safety of the locker room before she allowed herself to cry.

She had told herself she could defend her title despite Meike's presence in the draw and, thanks to her blistering performance at the start of the match, she had put herself one set away from accomplishing her goal. Victory—at a major, over Meike, and against the wishes of all the people who wanted to see her lose—had been in sight. Then everything had fallen apart.

Meike's change in tactics hadn't come as a surprise. Her baseline game wasn't working in the first set. It was only logical she would resort to the more aggressive style of play Helen had seen her practicing on board the *Southern Star*. Yet, even though she knew what was coming, Helen had been unable to prevent the final result. Her most powerful weapon, her serve, had abandoned her, leaving her defenseless against Meike's relentless onslaught of return winners.

She sat in front of her locker and draped a towel over her head as she allowed her tears to fall. She had lost to Meike plenty of times before, but never like this. Not when she had been so certain she would win.

Margaret Wilson, Helen's opponent in the mixed doubles final and her partner in the doubles final, placed a hand on her shoulder. "Pull yourself together. You still have two more matches to play."

Despite her loss in the singles final, Helen had two more chances to win a title today. Two more chances to redeem herself.

"Give me five minutes. I'll be right as rain by the time we take the court."

"Can you speed it up a little?" Margaret looked over her shoulder as the locker room door opened and Meike and Liesel swept in. "You don't want Meike to see you cry, do you?"

Helen watched Meike cradle the trophy that could have—*should* have—been hers. She knew from experience that nothing could detract from the joy of a win like the misery of a vanquished opponent. Meike was the better player today. She deserved to enjoy the moment. So Helen plastered on a smile she hoped appeared more genuine than the one she had flashed at the net and joined Meike and Liesel in front of their lockers.

"Meike. Liesel."

Meike's smile dimmed a bit but, for the most part, remained in place. Liesel, on the other hand, made a face like she'd been sucking lemons and quickly made herself scarce.

"I didn't mean to disrupt your preparations for the doubles final," Helen said. "I just wanted to offer you my congratulations on your singles win. Again. I seem to be doing that a lot lately."

"Thank you." Meike's eyes flicked to the other side of the room, where Liesel and Margaret were holding a whispered conversation of their own. "I look forward to our next encounter."

Helen glanced at her watch. "You'll get your wish in about fifteen minutes."

Meike laughed. "That isn't the encounter I was referring to. You promised me a rematch, remember?"

Helen's win at poker had happened much too long ago to offer any consolation against the pain of today's loss. "I'm not so sure I should give you one."

"Why not?" Meike's frown at not getting her way was so endearing it almost managed to brighten Helen's dark mood.

"Based on today's performance, I might lose my shirt."

Meike lowered her voice. "Isn't that the point?"

Helen felt a flash of desire that made her feel hotter than she'd been at any time during the match. She could feel the wet cabbage leaf on her head turning to sauerkraut as Meike's eyes bore into hers. "I want to take you for a night on the town," she said, wondering how Meike would react to the wonders—and temptations—the Big Apple had to offer. "Will you be stopping in New York City on your way home?"

"I haven't checked the itinerary in a while. If I remember correctly, I think we plan to skirt the coast of Africa, come to shore in Portugal, and take the train from Lisbon to Berlin."

"Change your plans," Helen said forcefully. "There's more to life than tennis, remember? You should take some time to celebrate winning a major tournament instead of preparing for an event in the middle of nowhere. To the victor go the spoils. Let me spoil you."

"What do you have in mind?"

Helen saw curiosity—and perhaps something more—in Meike's eyes.

"We could get a room at the Waldorf Astoria, order one of their famous namesake salads, cut into some big, juicy steaks, and top off the meal with a hearty slice of apple pie. Then I could take you to see Bill 'Bojangles' Robinson tap dance at the Cotton Club, or if you're up for it, I could take you someplace else. Someplace we could really let our hair down. Someplace a woman in a suit or a man in a dress wouldn't raise any eyebrows. What do you say?"

"I would love to, but I'm expected to be in—I'm expected at home on a certain date."

Helen made note of Meike's hesitation but decided not to call attention to it. For the moment, anyway. "You're a big girl. I'm sure your family would understand if you're a few days late." But she was beginning to wonder if Meike's parents were the only ones anxiously waiting for her to return from her long trip abroad. "There'll be plenty of time for family reunions later, champ. Let me show you a good time first."

"And if I say no?"

"Why would you want to?" Helen slid the back of her hand along the line of Meike's jaw. Meike's face glowed with the thrill of victory and the rush of arousal. She was even lovelier than usual in moments like this. Helen wanted to kiss her, but she didn't dare. Not here. Not now. Perhaps in New York, where they could be free to be themselves. If she didn't give Lanier the information he wanted, she might never feel free again. This could be her last chance. Her only chance.

"Why, indeed?"

Meike's smile almost made Helen's heart stop. Now all she needed to do was figure out a way to keep her heart from getting broken.

Chapter Five

February 1938
New York City

With Helen's help, Meike was able to exchange her ticket to Lisbon for one to London by way of New York. The new route meant it would take her longer to arrive in Berlin, but she was in no rush to get there anyway. What was there to go home to? Going home meant she wouldn't have Oskar glued to her side, but it didn't mean the surveillance of her would come to an end. After she arrived in Germany, agents would monitor her comings and goings from a distance. Far enough away to give her a semblance of freedom but close enough to be able to take away her liberty whenever they chose. For the past month, freedom had been a reality instead of an illusion. She wasn't looking forward to having it disappear.

She had waited until the last possible moment to tell Oskar, Inge, and Liesel about the change in her travel plans. Waited until there was nothing Oskar could do to change what she and Helen had already set in motion.

Standing in front of the floor-length mirror in the two-bedroom suite she and Helen had reserved at the Waldorf Astoria Hotel, she smiled as she remembered the look on Oskar's face when he realized she had outfoxed him. When she finally returned to Germany, she knew he would do everything in his power to make her pay for getting the best of him. No matter. During the long ocean voyage from Australia to the United States, she'd had plenty of time to devise her defense. If he tried to make life difficult for her, she intended to return the favor.

Winning the Australian Championships had given her a modicum of leverage and she intended to use it. Oskar, she could argue, was a distraction. Not just to her but to Liesel as well. In Adelaide, she and Liesel had lost the doubles final to Helen and her partner in straight sets. The first set had been close, but the second had been a runaway. Instead of strategizing with Meike to figure out a way to reverse their fortunes, Liesel had spent most of the second stanza staring into the stands to gauge Oskar's reaction to her poor play.

"Do you think Oskar's handsome?" Liesel had asked as the match began to slip irretrievably from their grasp.

"I really couldn't say," Meike had said, thrown by the non sequitur. "He isn't my type."

"Well, he's certainly mine."

Focused on her unsuccessful attempt at mounting a comeback in the match, Meike had almost forgotten about the exchange. Now, however, she intended to use it to her advantage.

Oskar appeared to have a soft spot for Liesel, and she was obviously harboring a crush on him. When she returned home, Meike planned to tell the officials of the German Tennis Association—and the ones of the National Socialist Party, for that matter—that if Oskar wasn't assigned to "accompany" someone else during their travels abroad, she would stop playing doubles with Liesel and find another partner. Preferably one from a country opposed to the Austrian's way of thinking. Since she and Liesel were Germany's top women's doubles team, she thought reassigning Oskar was the obvious choice. Time would tell if the officials would see things her way.

While Meike was putting the finishing touches on her makeup, Helen knocked on the bedroom door and poked her head inside. "Ready, champ?"

Meike turned to face her. She had expected Helen to be wearing a tuxedo or one of the many man-tailored suits she had sported on board the *Southern Star* on the way to and from Australia. Helen was wearing an evening gown instead. A cream-colored one that clung to her athletic body and perfectly complemented her tanned skin. Diamond studs glittered in her ears and a matching choker circled her neck. Helen looked vaguely uncomfortable, which meant the outfit was probably for propriety's sake, as was Swifty Anderson's expected presence at dinner. Once dinner was over, however, Meike doubted Helen would continue to abide by society's rules. Or was that only wishful thinking on her part?

"You look beautiful, Helen."

"You don't have to sound so surprised. If Friedrich can look good in a dress, why can't I?"

Meike laughed. "Isn't it rich? Two of the people who mean the most to me are a man who wears dresses and a woman who prefers suits."

"But not tonight."

"No," Meike said, giving Helen's sleek form another long, admiring look, "not tonight."

A spot of color bloomed in the hollow of Helen's throat. Meike wanted to sink her tongue into the depression and feel the heat. Taste Helen's skin. Hear her breath catch when—

"Shall we go?" Helen asked, forcing Meike to put her growing desire in check.

"So soon?" Meike had told herself once that she and Helen had no future. If she believed that, why couldn't she stop thinking about the past?"

"Swifty already snagged us a table. The best seats in the house. Or so he says."

Meike followed Helen to the elevator, where the uniformed operator welcomed them with a broad smile and a tip of his cap. "Welcome to New York, ladies."

Meike had been to New York City several times before. She used it as an embarkation point as she made her way to Forest Hills to compete in the US Championships each year. On this trip, however, she felt as wide-eyed as she had been on her first visit. She found herself amazed by the hustle and bustle of the busy city, the legions of tall buildings that seemed to scrape the sky, and, most of all, the woman who had invited her here in the first place.

She thought she had grown immune to Helen's charms. What was it about her that proved so hard to resist? Was it her wit, her ebullient personality, or her androgynous beauty? Perhaps, Meike thought with a sigh, it was all those things and more. Helen touched a place in her no one else had been able to reach. Before or since.

When the elevator car reached the first floor, the operator lifted the protective gate and opened the heavy steel doors. "Have a good evening, ladies."

Meike and Helen stepped into the well-appointed lobby, their heels clicking on the polished marble floor.

"The restaurant is—"

A nondescript man in a boxy brown suit stepped in front of Helen before she could finish her sentence. Startled, Helen took a step back. Her hand fluttered over her undoubtedly racing heart. The man grew instantly apologetic.

"I didn't mean to startle you, Miss Wheeler, but I'm a big fan of yours. May I have your autograph?"

He thrust a pen and a small piece of paper toward Helen. The paper had writing on it, but the words were too small for Meike to read, though she doubted they were important if the man was asking Helen to scribble her name over them. She noticed Helen's hand was shaking when she reached for the proffered pen. Hers undoubtedly would have been as well.

"Who should I make it out to?" Helen asked.

Obviously starstruck, the man faltered as if he couldn't remember his own name. "To Paul."

Helen glanced at the slip of paper and hastily signed her name. "Here you go, Paul. Thanks for being a fan."

"Thank *you*, Miss Wheeler. Bad luck in Adelaide, but better luck next time."

Helen mustered a half-hearted smile. "From your mouth to God's ears."

"It was nice meeting you, Miss Wheeler. You, too, Miss von Bismarck."

Paul finally glanced in Meike's direction. Until then, he'd only had eyes for Helen. Meike nodded an acknowledgment of his greeting but didn't speak. His adoration for Helen made any words from her unnecessary.

"I need a drink," Helen said once she and Meike were alone.

"Does that happen often?"

"More than you might think." Helen adjusted the wrap covering her muscular shoulders, making Meike long for another round of strip poker. This time with a much different ending. This time she wanted the show to continue all the way to the end instead of having the curtain come down before the final act was over. "Let's find our table before Swifty guzzles all the champagne."

Swifty stood when he saw them approach. Clearing his throat as if preparing to give a speech, he straightened his silk tie and raised his glass in a toast. "To the best—and prettiest— tennis players I have ever met."

"Aw, Swifty, you say the sweetest things."

"If I haven't told you before, Mr. Anderson, you certainly have a way with words."

He bowed so low his forehead nearly touched the cloth-covered table. "One of my many charms."

After Meike and Helen took their seats, the waiter brought out three Waldorf salads. Meike loved the contrast between the dish's various ingredients—the leafy greens, the crunchy walnuts, the tart apples, and the citrus-accented dressing. The appetizer was so good she hoped the entrée wouldn't suffer in comparison.

"When is your next tournament?" Helen asked after the salad plates were cleared but before the main course arrived.

Until this season, Meike typically began her year with a small indoor event held at the Rot-Weiss Tennis Club in Berlin. But this year was different. This year was about making history. Because this year could be her last.

"I'm entered in an event near the French Riviera next month." She hoped Friedrich would accompany her on the trip. She hoped even more fervently she could convince him to stay once he arrived. "What about you?"

"I'm heading home for the West Coast swing. After I play a few hard court tournaments and give several celebrities free tennis lessons, I'll come back East in a few months to sail to Europe for the clay court season."

"After tonight, I suppose I won't see you again until the French Championships." The thought made Meike almost unbearably sad. She didn't have many friends on tour. Helen was one of them. And at one time, she had been much, much more.

"Depending on my draw," Helen said with a chuckle, "you might not see me even then. In Paris, my shopping excursions usually last longer than my tournament runs."

"True, you haven't made it to the later stages of the French Championships in a few years, but you're a fine clay court player when you set your mind to it."

"I have my moments on clay, but not nearly enough of them for my taste."

"Does that mean you'll be skipping the Confederation Cup?"

The inaugural event was scheduled to be held on the slow red clay of Roland Garros the week after the French Championships, when most players' attention would have turned from clay to grass. The tournament's organizers were touting it as an event that would decide the best tennis nation in the world, but Meike doubted the best players would take part with Wimbledon, the real world championship, looming on the horizon.

"Clay may be my least favorite surface," Helen said, "but I can't pass up an opportunity to represent my country."

"Even if it hurts your chances at winning Wimbledon?" Meike expected to be tired after another grueling run at the French Championships and wanted to be sure she got as much rest as possible before she attempted to defend her Wimbledon title two short weeks after the French Championships ended. Let the Aussies and the Americans battle for world supremacy at the Confederation Cup. She had other goals in mind.

"Some things are more important than individual success. The Confederation Cup is one of them."

Helen's passion was admirable, but it didn't change Meike's mind about skipping the tournament. "Good luck to you and your team. I shall be rooting for you from the sidelines."

"I'd rather see you across the net. The Confederation Cup won't have the same relevance if the top-ranked player doesn't participate."

Meike looked away, unable to bear the disappointment in Helen's eyes. "Perhaps, but surely you can understand why I'm not too keen on wrapping myself in the flag these days. I don't want to make political statements. I just want to play tennis."

"You have no choice. Hitler's made you the face of the new Germany."

"I didn't ask him to and he certainly didn't ask my permission." The reminder that her name and face were being used to promote the ideals of a regime she didn't support made the sweet champagne turn to vinegar in Meike's mouth. "I thought you invited me to New York to have fun, not discuss politics."

"I did. So let's stop debating and start celebrating." Helen raised her arm to catch the waiter's attention. "Another bottle of champagne."

Meike emptied her glass. "Make that two."

❖

Helen knew Agent Lanier expected her to check in with him as soon as she stepped off the boat from Adelaide, but she hadn't expected to see him tonight. She had nearly screamed when he suddenly approached her outside the elevator. The note he had slipped her—the piece of paper he had shoved at her under the guise of asking for her autograph—had contained directions to a warehouse near the docks and asked her to meet him there tomorrow morning at eight "for training." She had memorized the directions and returned the note, but she had no idea what kind of training he had in mind.

The mystery had preoccupied her throughout dinner, leaving her unable to hold up her end of the conversation once talk turned from tennis to more mundane subjects. Thankfully, though, Swifty was there to take up her slack. But now the meal was almost over and she wouldn't have Swifty to hide behind for much longer.

"What are your plans for the night?" he asked.

"I figured we'd start at the Cotton Club, then play the rest of the evening by ear. I have two possible destinations in mind, but I'll let the champ decide which one we choose."

"Oh, no," Meike said. "You know the city far better than I do. Tonight, I'm in your hands."

The thought gave Helen an undeniable thrill. "Careful, Meike. You never know where my hands might end up."

"No, but I have a pretty good idea."

Meike's voice was a gentle purr that made Helen feel warm despite the cold glass of champagne in her hand. Swifty's cheeks reddened as if he felt the heat. He hurriedly pushed his chair away from the table. "I think that's my cue to leave. A pleasure, as always." He kissed the back of Meike's hand, then turned to Helen. "I would say, 'Don't do anything I wouldn't do,' but I don't feel like wasting my breath. Just be careful, okay?"

"Aren't I always?" The bubbles in the champagne were making Helen light-headed. She needed to keep her wits about her, but it didn't seem worth the effort. None of this was real. Her pursuit of Meike was all for show. A ruse to help the government get the information it needed to prevent a war. But why did it feel so genuine?

Swifty pressed his lips together like a disapproving schoolmarm. "Do you really want me to answer that?"

"No, I don't." Helen laughed despite her uncertainty. "Good night, Swifty. I'll meet you at the train station tomorrow morning."

"What do you mean you'll meet me? I thought we were sharing a taxi."

"Change of plans. I have to see Meike off. Then I have an errand to run."

"What kind of errand?" Swifty raised a speculative eyebrow. "The kind you need me to dish out a couple of sawbucks to clean up?"

"No, this one I can handle myself. For free."

At least she hoped so. She expected Lanier to exact a steep price from her tomorrow, but she doubted it would be monetary. Perhaps the training session he had planned for her wouldn't be as bad as she thought. Perhaps he only meant to give her typing lessons or teach her shorthand to speed up production of the weekly reports she had fallen behind on. Perhaps he didn't have anything physical in mind. She depended on her body to make a living. Her athletic ability was her greatest and, some would say, only asset. Surely Lanier and, by extension Uncle Sam, wouldn't put her career at risk by asking her to do something

YOLANDA WALLACE

foolish. Then again, they had potentially asked her to risk her life by keeping tabs on the Nazis. Why wouldn't they ask her to risk her livelihood, too?

"Let's go," she said after she signed for the meal. "The car should be ready."

Meike dragged her feet. "Don't you want to change clothes first?"

Helen continued outside, where a chauffeur and limousine were waiting. "What would you prefer me to wear?"

"I would prefer you to be comfortable."

"Aside from the shoes, I am." In truth, Helen would have preferred going upstairs and changing out of her dress into a suit, but, still recovering from their last encounter, she didn't want to risk running into Lanier again. She knew they were supposed to be on the same side, but sometimes it felt like they had different agendas. Tonight, she didn't want to think about the mission. Tonight, she just wanted to enjoy being with Meike, even though she couldn't tell if what was happening between them was imagined or real. "But don't worry about me," she said, ignoring the complaints her feet were making about the heels she had forced on them. "I'll be off my feet soon enough."

"Where to?" the chauffeur asked after Helen and Meike climbed into the back of the limousine.

"The Cotton Club."

"I have read about this place," Meike said as the chauffeur began to weave through traffic. "Isn't the Cotton Club the establishment where the audience is white but all the performers are black?"

"Yes," Helen said warily. She started to point out that, despite its policies, the Cotton Club was also one of the most famous nightclubs in New York, but it seemed too weak a rejoinder to counter Meike's argument.

"That hardly seems fair." Meike frowned at the obvious injustice of the entertainers' friends and families not being able to watch them take the stage and the entertainers themselves not being allowed to mingle with the crowds who paid dearly to watch them perform.

"I don't make the rules. I only follow them. Occasionally."

"Do you intend to follow the rules tonight?"

Helen took a long look at her. Was that lust she saw on Meike's face or were the three bottles of champagne they and Swifty had shared at dinner responsible for the rosy glow? "I intend to make them up as we go along."

She slowly reached under Meike's evening gown and slid a hand along her calf. Meike's skin was the color of marble and felt just as smooth. The heat of it seared Helen's palm. Meike responded to her touch with a high-pitched gasp that quickly dissolved into a low moan. Craving more, Helen moved her hand higher. When she met Meike's eyes, there was no mistaking what she saw. Meike wanted her. Still.

The liveried chauffeur was watching the traffic instead of his passengers, so Helen moved closer to Meike. She had been unable to press her advantage in Adelaide, but they were playing a much different game now. Now they weren't playing for a trophy. Now they were playing for keeps.

Helen slipped one hand between Meike's knees and caressed the soft skin of her inner thigh. With the other, she cradled the back of Meike's neck as Meike's eyelids slid shut and her head lolled on the seat rest.

"I want to kiss you," Helen whispered as she watched Meike fight a losing battle with her self-control. A fight she was ready to surrender as well.

"What's stopping you?"

Meike's question was a challenge. One Helen was unwilling to accept. She didn't want a quick grope in the backseat of a car. She no longer wanted to exact revenge for past slights. She wanted something more profound. Something real. A relationship built on honesty instead of the lies and half-truths her mission forced her to tell. But did Meike want the same thing? Did Meike want to be with her for the long run or just for one night?

"Am I serious enough for you, or do you still think I'm too frivolous to take a chance on?"

Meike's lips parted. Her eyes searched hers, seeking answers without, tellingly, offering any of her own. "None of that matters right now. Kiss me, Helen."

"In time."

Helen trailed a finger over Meike's lips and moved away, struggling to rein in her desire—and keep her priorities in order. She was supposed to be trying to win Meike's heart while keeping her own at a safe remove. She was supposed to remain objective while pretending to be anything but. But the closer she pretended to feel to Meike, the closer to her she actually felt.

When she kissed Meike, she wanted it to be real, not part of an act. But the more time she spent trying to dig up the dirt Lanier wanted, the less she knew what was real and what wasn't. Soon, she feared, she might not be able to tell the difference. If that happened, the battle might be won, but the war would be lost. Was fulfilling her duty worth losing her soul?

❖

Meike heard the Cotton Club before she saw it. Jaunty jazz music greeted her ears many minutes before she spotted the brilliantly lit sign hanging above the famed nightclub's front door. The club was opened by heavyweight boxing champion Jack Johnson in 1920 and was later run by gangster Owney Madden. It was in less infamous hands now, but Meike still felt an illicit thrill at the thought of going inside.

When the chauffeur pulled up to the curb, a long line of well-dressed patrons stood outside seeking entrance. The semicircular canopy overhead protected those at the front of the line from falling snow, but not from the driving wind whipping at the flags on neighboring buildings. Meike wondered how long the people in line had been standing in the cold—and how long she and Helen would be forced to join them. But when the chauffeur opened the door, Helen led her past the long queue and steered her toward the tuxedoed employee stationed next to the velvet rope stretched in front of the club's entrance.

"Good evening, Miss Wheeler," the man said with a smile as he unhooked the rope. "Welcome back."

"Thank you, Bobby." Helen slipped a folded bill into his pocket and gave him a friendly pat on the shoulder. "Get a little something for the wife and kids on your way home."

"Thank you, Miss Wheeler. I'll do that. Nick will show you to your usual table. Have a good evening."

"I'm sure I will."

"Do you come here often?" Meike asked after she and Helen took their seats at a table so close to the stage Meike almost felt like she was one of the performers instead of part of the audience.

"Not very," Helen said, though her mischievous smile hinted her response was less than honest. She took a sip of the champagne that had been chilled and waiting for them when they arrived, then nodded a greeting at one of the chorus girls kicking up her heels onstage.

"Do you know her?"

"Very well." This time, Helen's smile held an air of mystery. A mystery Meike was eager to unravel. "If you like, I'll introduce you to her after the show."

"I thought the entertainers weren't allowed to mingle with the patrons."

"They aren't. Most of the entertainers get together after the club closes. They drink peach brandy, smoke marijuana, and have informal jam sessions in the basement of the building next door. The superintendent lets them use the space and doesn't even charge them a fee. The outsiders lucky enough to get in are treated to an even better show than any of the ones put on here. The music isn't half-bad, either."

Meike couldn't imagine how what went on in the basement of a nondescript apartment building could possibly top what went on in the club itself. She gaped at the spectacle playing out onstage. Chorus girls—uniformly tall, light-skinned, and beautiful—danced to the driving beat provided by the tuxedo-clad musicians. The lavish stage sets were even more elaborate than the dancers' costumes. Meike felt like she was watching a Hollywood musical rather than a live show. She had never seen anything like it in person, not even in Berlin during its heyday.

When the chorus girls were done performing, they ceded the spotlight to a woman in a ruby red dress slit from ankle to mid-thigh. The woman idly fanned herself with a lacy white handkerchief between verses, but the songs she sang were so bawdy Meike felt like she was the one who needed cooling off.

Each act was better than the last. By the time Bill "Bojangles" Robinson took the stage, Meike doubted he could top everything that had come before. Seconds into his routine, however, she realized why he was billed as the headliner. His feet and legs moved so fast they were little more than dazzling blurs as he tap-danced across the stage. Meike was mesmerized. Until an unwelcomed visitor broke the spell.

"Uh oh," Helen said as a tipsy blonde lurched toward their table. The table tilted precariously as the woman leaned her weight on one end. Helen grabbed the bucket of champagne before it could slide to the floor. "Careful, Persephone. We wouldn't want to waste any of this, would we?"

Persephone grabbed the bottle and raised it to her lips. "Don't fret. I'll buy more," she said as she wiped droplets of champagne off her chin with the back of her gloved hand. "You said you would call me the next time you were in town. Why didn't you?"

"I've been busy."

"So I see." Persephone gave Meike a quick once-over, then barked a caustic laugh. "On my way over here, I thought she looked like me. Up close, though, she looks more like that kraut tennis player you lost to in Australia."

"She *is* that kraut tennis player I lost to in Australia."

"Seriously?"

Meike smiled after Persephone nearly choked on her pilfered champagne. "I could give you an autograph if you like."

"No, thank you. I think I'll tuck my tail between my legs and take my leave with as much dignity as I can muster instead."

"I take it you know her as well," Meike said after Persephone wobbled back to her own table.

"You're not jealous, are you?"

"Should I be?"

"As you reminded me on the *Southern Star*, we aren't together anymore. I'm free to spend time with whoever I choose." Helen's gaze seemed to penetrate to Meike's very soul. "Would you rather I spent time with only you?"

Tonight, Meike wanted nothing more. But her future was too uncertain to draw anyone into it. Even for one night. "We both know that's impossible, Helen."

The waiter approached the table carrying another bottle of champagne, but Helen waved him off.

"Then why are you here with me tonight? Why did you accept my invitation to come to New York if being with me is impossible?"

The pleasant buzz Meike had felt since leaving Adelaide faded as reality intruded on the fantasy world Helen had created for her. For a few blissful weeks, Helen had allowed her to live life as it used to be. As it probably never would be again. Now their time together was about to come to an end and she would be forced to mourn its passing once more.

"Because I would rather be here than home," she said before she could convince herself not to. "Because I would rather be here with you than anywhere else."

Helen's smile was tinged with sadness. She reached out and caressed Meike's cheek. Meike leaned into the pressure of Helen's hand, trying to take comfort in the solace Helen was offering even as Helen's words broke her heart.

"You're putting up a good front, Meike, but you're obviously not yourself. You haven't been since Oskar Henkel appeared in your life. Tonight is the first time in months I've seen more than mere flashes of the old you. The real you. The woman I once loved. I want her back, Meike. Tell me what I have to do to make her stay."

Meike closed her eyes. She was waging a war she couldn't hope to win. Her rekindled feelings for Helen were becoming too powerful to resist, but the Nazis' grip on her life was too strong to overcome. She was so tired of fighting. Maybe she should take the path of least resistance. Maybe she should just give in. If she did, perhaps she could stay alive long enough for the miracle she constantly prayed for to finally occur.

She pushed Helen's hand away, even though her body yearned for her touch. "It's too late, Helen. The woman you loved is already gone."

CHAPTER SIX

February 1938
New York City

Helen ran along the pier, mirroring the ship's slow but steady progress as the *Ocean Voyager* left the harbor. In the growing distance, the white handkerchief Meike waved on deck looked like a flag of surrender.

"I'll see you soon," Helen yelled, though she doubted Meike could hear her over the cries of the hundreds of people the departing passengers had left behind. She let her hand drop after she ran out of real estate and Meike moved farther out of reach. "Be safe."

As Meike steamed toward home, Helen wondered what was next for both of them. The night before, she had offered Meike a chance to ease the obvious burden she carried, and Meike had seemed eager to take her up on her offer, but something had held her back. Not something. Someone.

Meike had been her old self after they ditched Oskar Henkel in Adelaide and sailed to New York together. She had been relaxed and happy and receptive to Helen's advances. Just like old times. Then, when Helen thought she was finally making progress, Meike had pushed her away. Meike's demeanor had changed as soon as Helen mentioned Oskar Henkel's name.

Henkel discomfited Meike. That much was clear. The question was why. Helen had a theory. And it involved Gottfried von Cramm. She had heard rumors the Nazis were making life miserable for him. When he was in Germany, they followed him everywhere he went, trying to catch him committing a homosexual act. They didn't seem to care he was gay when he was winning every tournament in sight. After he suffered back-to-back losses to Don Budge at Wimbledon and the Davis Cup, however, they seemed determined to put him away. Perhaps for good. If Meike was being given the same treatment as Gottfried, the surveillance on her was much more overt than it was on him. The pressure to succeed, however, must have been even more intense. Since Gottfried had failed to bring home a title at Wimbledon or the Davis Cup, the two most important competitions in men's amateur tennis, Meike had no option but to succeed. No wonder winning seemed more like a relief for her than a cause for celebration.

Helen wanted to save Meike from the Nazis' clutches, but she didn't know how. If they wanted to punish Meike for being a lesbian, Helen's pursuit of her could put her in more danger. It could also jeopardize her mission. How was she supposed to get what Lanier wanted without putting both her and Meike's lives at risk?

She hailed a cab, gave the driver the address she had memorized from Lanier's note, and used the ride across town to try to figure out her next move. Lanier had asked her to gather information, but he hadn't said what he planned to do with it. Would he take action if she told him she thought Meike was in danger, or would he sit on the sidelines and do nothing until she had proof? By then, it could be too late. For Meike and for her.

After the cabbie dropped her off at the warehouse where Lanier had asked her to meet him, Helen pushed the door open and cautiously looked inside. She saw crates and boxes everywhere, but no sign of life. Had she come to the wrong place or had she been lured into a trap?

"Hello?"

Her voice echoed off the high ceilings. The skylight overhead let the morning light stream in, but she felt little of its warmth. She shivered, though she couldn't tell if it was because of the frigid temperature or the cold fingers of fear dancing up her spine. She froze when she heard footsteps thudding on the concrete floor.

"Hello?" she called again.

Lanier stepped into the open. "You made it," he said, leaning on a neatly stacked column of crates marked *Fragile—Handle with Care*.

Helen loosened her grip on the lapels of her coat as anger replaced her trepidation. "Were you trying to blow my cover last night or do you simply enjoy putting me on the spot?"

Lanier shoved his hands in his pockets like he was taking a stroll in the park instead of putting her through the wringer. "Last night was a test. I wanted to see how you would react to being caught by surprise."

"Did I pass?"

Her voice dripped sarcasm, but Lanier either didn't detect it or chose to ignore it. "With flying colors. Now tell me what you've learned."

"Nothing yet. Nothing you can use, anyway."

Lanier looked skeptical. "Try me."

"What do you want me to say?" Even though she didn't have anything to report, she didn't want him to think she wasn't making an effort. She was trying. She really was, but she seemed to be spinning her wheels instead of gaining traction. "I can't force Meike to talk to me if she doesn't want to."

When she first met Lanier, she had thought he was nothing more than a harmless pencil pusher in a cheap suit. When he took a step toward her, he seemed much more dangerous than she'd previously given him credit for.

"Sometimes what people don't say is more important than what they do. Like now, for instance. I need you to realize

I'm your ally, Helen, not your enemy. I want you to trust me. And above all, I want you to know I'm not stupid. Meike von Bismarck traveled to Adelaide with one of Heinrich Himmler's hand-picked flunkies and you don't think that was information I could use?"

"Oskar Henkel is associated with Hitler's right-hand man? He works for Heinrich Himmler, the head of the Gestapo?"

"You mean you didn't know?"

"All I knew was Meike was afraid of him, but I didn't know why."

Lanier cocked his head. "Is it Henkel she fears or the thought of you unearthing the truth behind her connection to him? Like I told you before, she is a part of Hitler's inner circle. He might not stoop to sharing troop movements with her, but I know he's told her something. He likes to brag too much and he's too obsessed with blue-eyed blondes not to try to impress her with his power. If he's taken her into his confidence—or his bed—I want to know."

Helen balled her hands into fists, ready to fight to defend Meike's honor. "First of all, Meike would never let him touch her, no matter what was at stake. And, second, she wouldn't lie to me."

"You're lying to her, aren't you, or did you tell her the real reason you decided not to turn pro?"

Helen's stomach soured. She hated the thought of lying to Meike, someone who embodied honesty and integrity more than anyone she had ever met. On the court, Meike was known to give away not just a point but an entire game if a linesman's call erroneously went in her favor. Off the court, she was just as forthright, her moral compass directed toward true north. If Helen told Meike the real reason she had come back into her life, would she understand why or would she consider the deceit an unforgivable offense?

"I'm lying because I have to, Agent Lanier, not because I want to. It's different." But she doubted Meike would see it that way.

"How is it different? She could be having a similar conversation with her own handler as soon as she reaches Berlin."

"Meike isn't a spy."

"I'm sure, if given a chance, she would say the same about you. You're keeping a secret from her. Why is it so hard for you to believe she might be keeping one from you, too?"

"Because I know her. What the Nazis believe and what she stands for are polar opposites. Their beliefs are not hers."

"People change. And sometimes they're willing to put aside their beliefs in order to survive."

Helen replayed the conversations she and Meike had shared on the way to Adelaide and on the way back to New York, searching in vain for some subtle sign that would lead her to believe Meike wasn't who she appeared to be.

"Why didn't Henkel accompany her to New York?" Lanier asked.

"Because I helped her give him the slip."

Lanier tapped his chin thoughtfully. "If she's as innocent as you say she is, she could hear about that when she gets home."

"That's what I'm afraid of." Lanier looked at her for so long, Helen grew uncomfortable under his gaze. "What is it?"

"You have feelings for her, don't you?"

Helen stiffened. "I'm playing a part you asked me to play."

"And you're playing it well."

Helen didn't know whether to take his comment on her skill at being deceitful as a compliment or an insult. "Now that we've established my acting bona fides, may I leave now? I have a train to catch."

"Not for a few hours yet, you don't. You didn't think I dragged you all the way down here just to chat, did you?"

"Then why am I here?"

"Come with me."

After following him into the maze of crates, she paused when she saw a man with thighs like tree trunks and biceps the size of her head standing in the center of the maze.

"This is Floyd," Lanier said. "He'll be your instructor."

Floyd was so big he practically blocked out the sun, a skill Helen doubted she would be able to learn. "No offense, but what do you plan on having him teach me?"

"Everything from how to handle a gun to how to defend yourself during hand-to-hand combat."

"Wait." Helen balked after she imagined Floyd tossing her around on the dirty mattress at his feet. Was that dried blood or rust stains dotting the soiled material? She decided she was better off not knowing. "I didn't sign up for this."

"No, you didn't," Lanier said. "You volunteered."

"Today's session is the first of many," Floyd said. "You and I are going to be best friends by the time we're done. Where shall we begin?"

When he cracked his knuckles, it sounded like bones breaking. Helen hoped it wouldn't be a harbinger of the future. She pointed toward the paper target taped to a nearby hay bale. "How about some target practice? That can't be too painful."

"Unless the gun blows up in your hand," Floyd said as he stepped off the mattress and beckoned her toward a sheet-covered table. Helen couldn't tell if he was joking or serious about the exploding pistol and decided it was probably better for her peace of mind if she didn't ask. He pulled the sheet aside to reveal an assortment of handguns. "Try them on for size and see which one appeals to you."

Helen felt like Goldilocks. The first gun she picked up was too heavy and the second too light. The third, naturally, felt just right. "How about this one?"

"Good choice." The gun wasn't much bigger than Helen's hand, but it looked miniscule when Floyd cradled it in his massive mitt. "It's a twenty-five caliber automatic with a six-shot clip. It's light, accurate at close range, and easy to hide." He returned the gun to her. "If you don't want to secure it in a shoulder holster that would conceal it under your arm, you can stash it in your clutch bag when you're out on the town."

He took a few mincing steps but stopped the garish pantomime when she glared at him to show she didn't find his attempt at humor very amusing. "I don't know about you, but I don't make it a habit to frequent places where I need to pack a pistol."

He held up his hands in surrender. "I didn't mean any offense, ma'am, but Europe isn't as peaceful as it once was. If you're thinking of traveling there this spring, I wouldn't board the boat without it. Not if you're planning to take on the Nazis in their own backyard."

Helen's fear returned in spades. The mission Lanier had asked her to take on suddenly seemed much more dangerous than she had anticipated.

After Floyd showed her how to load, clean, and oil the gun, he finally got around to teaching her how to fire it.

"Don't pull the trigger. Squeeze it. If you snatch at the trigger, you'll jerk the barrel of the gun away from your target. If you've gone to the trouble of pointing a gun at something, chances are you want to hit what you're aiming at. If someone gets after you, aim for his body and keep firing until he goes down."

Helen pointed the barrel of the gun at the paper target fifteen feet away. She took several deep breaths to slow her racing heart. If she was this nervous taking on a paper target, how would she be able to shoot at a live one? A paper target was harmless. A live one could shoot back.

Her first shot went wide and slammed into the warehouse wall. Her second was closer, but still nowhere near the target. The third, at least, managed to hit the hay.

"You're getting closer," Floyd said, offering encouragement. "Just breathe and squeeze. Breathe and squeeze."

She took a deep breath, slowly exhaled, and gently squeezed the trigger. She let out a gasp of surprise when the bullet hit the center of the target. She took another shot to make sure the previous one wasn't a result of dumb luck. That shot struck the center of the bull's-eye, too.

"Paul was right," Floyd said. "You are a natural."

Helen smiled at the compliment—and the unexpected sense of accomplishment. "What's next?"

They shot at the paper target for another half hour or so, then Floyd pulled out a cardboard silhouette and taught her how to shoot at something that looked more like a person instead of a target. She effortlessly shot holes in the areas that corresponded to the head, heart, and stomach.

"Good job," Floyd said. "Do you think you'd be able to shoot at the real thing just as easily?"

"We'll see," she said, but she hoped she'd never get the chance to find out.

"We'll wrap up today's session with some self-defense training. Here's a change of clothes."

With the smell of gun smoke heavy in the air, Floyd tossed her a pair of gray sweatpants and a matching sweatshirt that appeared to be at least two sizes too big.

"Where are the shoes?"

"You won't need them. Get changed and meet me on the mattress. You don't have anything I haven't seen before, but you can duck behind some of the crates if you're shy."

Accustomed to walking around crowded locker rooms in various states of undress, Helen wasn't especially modest. Remaining where she was, she exchanged her clothes for the ones Floyd had provided and rolled up the sleeves of the sweatshirt a few times so she would look less like a kid playing dress-up in her big brother's clothes.

"This isn't what I would call a fair fight," she said after she joined Floyd on the mattress. "You're almost a foot taller than I am and probably outweigh me by a hundred pounds."

"It isn't the size of the dog in the fight. It's the size of the fight in the dog. You see my size as an advantage, but I'm going to teach you how to use it against me. Put your hands up."

She did as he asked, expecting him to tell her what was about to come next. She screamed in fright when he grabbed her arm, tossed her over his shoulder, and sent her flying through the air. She landed hard on the mattress and remained motionless until she could breathe without pain.

"Lesson one: never let your guard down." Floyd held out a hand and helped her to her feet. "Are you ready for lesson two?"

"That depends." Helen rubbed her aching tailbone. "Is it as painful as the first?"

Floyd grinned. "You'll thank me when I'm done."

By the time they were done grappling, she felt like cursing him instead. Every muscle she had was sore, her arms were covered in bruises, and her throat ached from Floyd's "accidental" karate chop to her windpipe. She had never endured such a strenuous workout. And today was only the first day.

"I think it's time to stop," Lanier said from his spot on the sidelines after Floyd taught her how to gouge out someone's eyes. "You can't fit three weeks of training into one day."

"I'm leaving for California in a few hours. Unless you plan on following me there, today is the last day we're going to have for a while."

Floyd put his hands on his hips. "She's right, Paul. She'll be playing in Europe for most of the spring. We need to take advantage of the time we have."

Outvoted two to one, Lanier reluctantly conceded defeat. "If you insist."

Grinning like a schoolboy at recess, Floyd came at her in a rush. Helen kept her hands up like he had taught her, crouched low, grabbed his arm in both of hers, and tossed him over her shoulder. He landed in a heap, but her technique must have been off because she heard something pop. Then she felt searing pain in her shoulder. Her right shoulder. Her serving shoulder. Her worst nightmare had come true. Just as she had feared, coming here today might have put her career at risk.

"Do you need a minute?" Floyd asked, his deep voice filled with concern.

Helen fought back tears as she cradled her injured arm. "No, what I need is a doctor."

❖

March 1938
Rheinsteifel, Germany

Meike fretted the entire journey home. She feared she would be detained the instant she set foot on German soil. But when she stepped off the train in Berlin, the Gestapo agents she had expected to see were not in evidence. The only person waiting for her was Friedrich.

"Meike!"

Friedrich looked upbeat, but he appeared to be wasting away. He had bags under his eyes, his lush brown hair had begun to thin, and he was skinnier than Meike had ever seen him. His once perfectly tailored suit drooped on his narrow frame. Almuth, the family cook, would have her work cut out for her trying to fatten him up before they left for France in two weeks' time.

"Darling Fritzi." Meike dropped her carry-on bags on the platform and ran toward Friedrich to give him a hug. The yellow Star of David pinned to the lapel of his coat scratched her cheek as he crushed her against his scrawny chest. "It's been much too long."

"Yes, it has." He held her at arm's length to take a long look at her. "You are, as the Americans say, a sight for sore eyes." He gave her shoulders a squeeze, then stooped to pick up the bags she had dropped. "Speaking of Americans," he said in a conspiratorial whisper, "I see you're spending time with yours again."

"Who, Helen?"

He pursed his lips in gentle admonishment. "Unless there are other Americans you're sleeping with that you haven't told me about."

As the porter trailed them through the station at a discreet distance, Meike wrapped her arm around Friedrich's and leaned her head toward his. How she had missed their gossip sessions. Catching up on everyone's activities. Teasing each other about their love lives and her decided lack of one. "I'm not sleeping with Helen."

"If you aren't, you should be. I've heard rave reviews about her performance. Mostly from you."

Meike squeezed his arm to remind him they weren't alone. And to warn him to keep the past where it belonged: in the past. "She and I are ancient history. Those who don't learn from history are destined to repeat it."

Friedrich glanced at the SS agents keeping a close eye on the passengers. Black-uniformed reminders of their country's inexorable path toward yet another world war. "Truer words were never spoken."

The porter placed Meike's luggage in the trunk of Friedrich's car and bowed after she tipped him a few marks for his efforts. "Thank you, Miss von Bismarck. Welcome home."

Meike thanked him, but she wouldn't be home—truly home—for several more hours yet. Friedrich opened the Phantom's passenger door for her, but an SS agent stepped into her path before she could climb inside.

"Your papers, please."

"My papers have already been examined." She showed him the stamp the customs agent had affixed to her passport when she crossed the border.

"Not yours. His." The agent turned to Friedrich and held out his hand. "Show me your papers, Jew." His breath reeked of alcohol as he barked the command. Meike guessed his request had more to do with showing his authority over someone he perceived to be inferior to him than performing his duty. "Friedrich Stern. What do you do for a living, Friedrich Stern?" he asked as he slowly read the requested documents.

"I was a...performer before my cabaret card was taken away."

"A performer, eh?" The agent turned to his equally inebriated companion and flashed him a cruel smile. "Boris and I could use some entertainment, couldn't we?" Boris shrugged noncommittally, seemingly more interested in scratching his crotch than participating in the conversation. "Why don't you perform for us now, Friedrich Stern?"

Boris swayed a little as he took a sip from an engraved silver flask Meike suspected hadn't been purchased but liberated from someone else's possessions. "We don't have time, Helmut," he said, finally giving his crotch a rest. "The girls are waiting for us at the beer garden."

Helmut waved off Boris's protests. "The girls will still be there when we arrive. When we get there, we can tell them all about the free show they missed." He tucked Friedrich's papers under his arm and clapped his hands like an eager audience member waiting for his favorite performer to take the stage. "Come on, Friedrich Stern. Sing me a song."

Instead of one of his trademark torch songs that never failed to bring tears to his listeners' eyes, Friedrich launched into a halting version of a song more popular in beer halls than cabarets. When he performed in drag on a beautifully lit stage, he sang in a rich soprano so pure few would believe he wasn't biologically female. Dressed like a man on a dirty city street, he sang in a much lower register, occasionally drifting—perhaps intentionally, Meike thought—off-key. Helmut stopped him after a few bars.

"No wonder you lost your cabaret card. Perhaps it's time you found another profession because you're obviously a piss poor singer." He tossed Friedrich's papers on the ground and urinated on them. "Now you have the papers to match," he said as he walked away, his and Boris's drunken laughter drifting on the wind.

Meike bent to retrieve the soiled papers, but Friedrich held out a hand to stop her. "Don't." He gathered the sodden documents between two fingers and held them in front of him as they dripped on the ground. "Get in the car."

Meike climbed inside the Rolls-Royce and closed the passenger door behind her. She felt like apologizing even though she knew she wasn't at fault. Friedrich didn't speak, but she could feel his fury as he stomped on the accelerator and directed the Phantom away from the site of his humiliation.

"I know it wasn't my best performance," he said after the streets of Berlin had disappeared from view, "but I didn't think it was *that* bad."

Meike laughed despite herself. Friedrich often used humor to defuse a tense situation. If he weren't careful, though, he could end up laughing all the way to an early grave. "How is Hans?" she asked, changing the subject to one she hoped would prove more pleasant.

Hans Strauss, an accountant from Frankfurt, was Friedrich's long-time and long-suffering lover, content to remain in the shadows while Friedrich basked in the spotlight. Friedrich's attention occasionally strayed as wealthy admirers lavished him with gifts and promises of a life Hans could never hope to provide, but his devotion to Hans never faltered. "He has fled to Switzerland."

Since Hans had relatives in Zurich, the news wasn't entirely unexpected, but Meike was surprised to hear he had decided to leave without Friedrich. Despite Friedrich's frequent affairs, Hans had never left his side. Until now. "Do you plan to join him?"

Friedrich's delicate hands tightened their grip on the steering wheel. "No."

"Why on earth not?"

"Tell me, Meike." He took his eyes off the road and turned to look at her. "Do you plan to leave Germany?"

"I can't leave. My family is here."

"So is mine." He took her hand in his and held it tight, reminding her that even though they weren't related by blood, they were still family. "Now tell me about your American."

"Helen is too independent to be anyone's anything. She isn't *my* American."

"She was once and I suspect you would like her to be again."

"I have enjoyed spending time with her the past few months, but what we had in the past is over. We are just friends now."

"Tell me again why you ended things."

Knowing he would see through a lie, Meike responded with the truth. "She got too close. I was afraid of losing to her."

Friedrich's once perfectly arched eyebrows had grown in full and thick, but they remained just as expressive. "You ended a promising relationship because you were afraid of losing a tennis match?"

Back then, the pressure to win was self-induced and not nearly as intense as it was now. And though it had been part of the reason Meike had decided to let Helen go, it hadn't been the only one.

"I was afraid of losing myself. When she and I were together, we felt like one being. I didn't know where I ended and she began. It was frightening."

"No, darling, it was love."

"It was an affair." Although applying the word to her relationship with Helen made their time together seem trivial, how else could she describe something that had been so temporary? "Being with her was like eating cotton candy. Enjoyable in small amounts, but not in large quantities. I loved being with her, and for a time, I thought I might even be in love with her, but even when we were together, I felt like we existed at the periphery of each other's lives instead of the center. Our respective careers got in the way."

"Tennis brought you together, but it also divided you."

"Yes, but it wasn't the only reason we parted. Helen and I have much in common, but we are fundamentally different. She lives for the present, Fritzi, not the future. I want a future with someone, not a few months or a few years of a relationship that will never amount to anything more than a pleasant diversion."

Yet, during their time together, Helen had touched her in a way no one ever had before or since. And not just sexually. Helen had made her laugh until her sides ached. Helen had made her scream until her throat was raw. And most of all, Helen had made her dream of a life that could never be. A life Helen didn't want and one she could no longer hope to have.

"She wanted a good time and you wanted forever. That's always the case with you." Friedrich patted her hand. "Beautiful dreamer, when will you realize forever isn't meant for people like us?"

Friedrich's question sent Meike into a funk she couldn't pull herself out of until the Phantom neared the freshwater lake the Swiss called Lake Constance but the Germans referred to as Bodensee. She rolled down the window and stuck her head outside the car, inhaling the crisp scent of the wind as it whipped across the cerulean water. She sighed contentedly, surrounded by the familiar sights and sounds of home.

After Friedrich maneuvered the car through the tight city streets of her hometown, he finally reached the grounds of her family estate. Flanked by the assorted cooks, maids, butlers, chauffeurs, and groundskeepers they employed, her parents waved to her from the front steps of the family castle, a sturdy stone structure that had been in von Bismarck hands for almost four centuries.

Meike looked at the lush green grass in the foreground and the snow-capped mountains in the distance. She and her younger brother Michael, who was away studying engineering at the University of Hamburg to avoid being conscripted to join the army, would inherit their parents' titles and property one day, but she doubted that day would come anytime soon. Her parents were only in their early fifties, and their parents, in turn, were as hale and hearty as ever even though all four were nearing eighty.

I might be known as the Countess on the tennis court, Meike thought with a smile, but it will be many years from now before I will be able to be called that at home.

"Mama. Papa." She hugged her parents one at a time.

When she was growing up, her father had been the more openly affectionate of the two. In recent years, however, as her travels kept her away from home for longer and longer periods of time, her mother had become more demonstrative. Today, her mother held on for so long Meike began to think she didn't intend to let go.

"How long will you be home this time?" her mother asked when she finally released her.

"For two weeks. Then I'll be heading to St. Tropez for a tournament. If I'm lucky, perhaps I can convince Friedrich to accompany me."

"Oh, that would be lovely. A trip to the Côte d'Azur would do you both good. Especially you, Friedrich. Come inside. You look like you could use a big bowl of Almuth's famous rabbit stew. We can talk between spoonfuls."

Friedrich shook Meike's father's hand, then offered her mother his arm. "I know better than to argue with such a charming hostess. Lead the way, Countess."

Meike's father clamped his pipe between his teeth as he and Meike supervised the butlers' offloading of her luggage from Friedrich's car. "How was your trip?"

"Long," she said with a weary sigh.

"But successful, I trust."

She grinned as she caught him examining her bags. Wondering, no doubt, which one contained the trophy she had earned for winning the Australian Championships. He seemed to take even more satisfaction in her victories than she did. He always listened intently as she recounted her results, requesting more and more details until telling him about her matches often lasted longer than the matches themselves.

"Are you looking for this?" She reached into her overnight bag and pulled out the sterling silver trophy she had received in Adelaide.

"Oh, my." Her father blew out an aromatic plume of smoke. "It is beautiful, Meike. May I?" After she handed him the trophy, he held it as hesitantly as a new father cradling his infant child for the first time.

For Meike, this was what winning was all about. Not earning accolades from fans or the press, but experiencing moments like this. Moments she spent watching pride light up her father's bright blue eyes.

He put an arm around her and pressed a kiss to her forehead. "Fritzi and Katja will keep each other entertained for hours as they debate hemlines and the latest Paris fashions. Why don't we retire to the study and have a glass of brandy by the fire?"

"Is something wrong, Papa?" Meike asked, noticing the fine lines of tension that had started to gather around his mouth after he suggested they spend some time alone.

He opened the heavy oak door and ushered her inside the study. Three of the four walls were covered by floor-to-ceiling bookcases filled with leather-bound books. The fourth featured a massive stone fireplace that served as the perfect location for roasting marshmallows or gathering in front of to tell scary stories. Two things Meike and her brother had done as often as possible when they were children but hadn't had time for in far too long.

Hildegard, the family's Russian wolfhound, lounged in front of the fireplace now. Meike bent and scratched the dog between the ears. "Hello, old girl."

Hildegard lifted her head and gave Meike a welcoming yip, then put her chin on her paws and returned to her nap. Meike wasn't put off by the less than enthusiastic greeting. Hildegard was almost seventeen. She didn't venture too far from her two favorite spots—the hearth and her food bowl—and didn't allow intrusions to either domain. Meike considered herself lucky her beloved childhood pet was still around to greet her at all.

Her father poured her a glass of brandy. "A telegram came for you while you were away. I didn't know if it might be good news or bad, and I was too afraid to open it and find out. So I held it for you until you returned." He pulled a sealed envelope from his pocket and handed it to her. "I thought you might like to read it in private so you wouldn't worry your mother."

"Thank you, Papa."

She hadn't told her family about all the threats the Nazis had made against her, but they knew Party members were trying to force her to join their ranks. And they knew how dangerous it was for her to refuse. She took the envelope with shaking hands.

Her father regarded her a moment, his eyes filled with concern. "Would you like me to stay?"

"No, Papa, I'll be fine."

She had kept the details of Hitler's edict to herself, wanting to bear the load alone like she did most burdens. But now she felt her knees begin to buckle from the added weight. She sat in a nearby armchair and, after she heard her father close the door behind him, she slid a finger under the envelope's flap and ripped it open. Her heart hammered in her chest as she removed the piece of paper inside. She had done everything the Nazis had asked. She had continued to win. So why didn't it feel like enough? Why did they keep asking for more?

She took another sip of brandy before she unfolded the telegram. She frowned in confusion when she saw the return address was New York City instead of Berlin. She didn't know anyone in New York City. No one except—

She lowered her gaze to the bottom of the page. The telegram was from Helen. When she was finished reading it, Meike felt like her father had when he had received it. She didn't know if it meant good news or bad.

"Meike?" Her father knocked on the door and poked his head inside the room. "May I come in?"

"Of course, Papa."

"Is everything all right?"

"I'm afraid not. Helen Wheeler has injured her shoulder and her doctors have suggested she take several weeks off to rest. If the joint doesn't heal on its own, she might require surgery. Then she could be out of commission for months instead of weeks. If she is fortunate enough to play at all."

Her father took a seat opposite her. "That is bad news. I have only seen her play a limited number of times in person. All on clay, which doesn't suit her game, but I enjoy her style of play. Very athletic and incredibly dynamic. The way she rushes to the net at every available opportunity, she puts me in mind of a female Don Budge."

Meike held up the telegram. "The way she describes her current situation in here, she might have to change the style of play you love so much."

"Do you think she can do it?"

"It is easier to change a baseliner into a serve-and-volleyer and vice versa when she is still a relative beginner. Once she becomes an established player, the task becomes much more difficult."

"Difficult, but not impossible." Meike's father took another puff on his pipe. He had always talked appreciatively of Helen's game and seemed genuinely distraught she might not ever be the player she once was. "She has the most powerful women's serve I have ever seen. It would be a shame if such a weapon were lost forever."

"Yes, that would be a shame." She remembered how rattled Helen had become when her serve began to falter in Adelaide. How would Helen react if she lost it for good? Would she be able to lift the rest of her game to compensate or would she slowly slide down the rankings, eventually relegated from a contender to a competitor filling out the field?

"You should invite her to come here."

"Here? Why?"

"Can you think of a better place to relax and recover? It is quiet, out of the way, and heaven knows we have the room."

Meike considered the idea but quickly dismissed it. "I have several tournaments lined up in the coming months. It would be rude of me to invite Helen to be somewhere I'm not."

"Even if you invited her today, it would take her several weeks to arrive, which means you could still play the tournament in St. Tropez, and you and Friedrich could have a brief holiday before you return."

"If I have my way, I will be returning from St. Tropez alone."

"Oh," her father said, unable to hide his surprise. "I doubt Fritzi would willingly leave the vast majority of his assets behind, which means you plan to smuggle the money to him." He leaned forward in his seat as if he planned to spring out of it at a moment's notice. "You could end up in prison, Meike."

"I could be imprisoned for a variety of offenses, Papa. Helping a friend is the least of my concerns."

"No wonder playing the tournament in St. Tropez is so important to you," her father said thoughtfully. "And all the more reason you should pull out of the ones that follow immediately after. You'll need time to gauge the government's reaction to Friedrich's departure—and to plan your next move if they come after you for helping him leave."

"Your idea is a good one, but I wouldn't want Helen to get caught in the middle if there are repercussions against me. Besides," she said, trying to lighten the mood, "I think she would prefer to recuperate on the beaches of California than here."

Her father swirled his snifter of brandy. "This is Castle von Bismarck. The Nazis wouldn't dare come for you here. You will always be safe inside these walls. So would she."

"Perhaps I will send her a telegram," Meike said, not wanting to admit to her father—or to herself—how much the idea appealed to her. Helen's invitation to spend time with her in New York had come as a surprise. No doubt Meike's return invitation would as well. But would it be as eagerly received? As their night at the Cotton Club had shown, Helen didn't lack for company. Would she be content to limit herself to Meike's for a few weeks?

Beautiful dreamer, Fritzi had said during the drive from Berlin, *when will you realize forever isn't meant for people like us?* Perhaps he and Helen had it right. Forever, Meike was forced to admit, wasn't promised to anyone. All she had was the present. She needed to live each moment as if it could be her last. Because it just might be.

The phone on the desk jangled. Startled, Meike's father cursed under his breath. He had never warmed to the modern convenience her mother had insisted on having installed in the foyer and the study, and he showed his displeasure now.

"How I hate that contraption. Carrier pigeons are more civilized and much less intrusive. Sure, they shit on everything in sight, but I would prefer the occasional soiled hat brim to the heart attack I have every time that infernal bell rings."

Meike's smile faded when she heard raised voices outside the study. She and her father rushed into the foyer, where Friedrich was holding Meike's weeping mother in his arms. Maria, the maid who usually answered the telephone when it rang, was ashen. The receiver dangled off the telephone table, the connection lost.

"What's wrong?" Meike asked. "Who was that on the line?"

"Gottfried von Cramm's mother." Meike knew what Friedrich would say next even before the words left his lips. "Gottfried has been arrested. Gestapo agents came to his house and took him away while he and his family were having after-dinner drinks in their salon."

"Arrested?" Meike's father asked. "On what charge?"

Meike knew there could be only two possibilities. Gottfried had either been taken in for being a homosexual or for smuggling money to his Jewish lover, Manasse Herbst, who had fled the country three years earlier and had been living in exile ever since.

"Jutta doesn't know," Meike's mother wailed. "The agents would only say they were taking him to Berlin. They gave him time to pack a few things, then they drove him away."

"What does this mean, Meike?" her father asked. "What does it mean for you?"

"I don't know, Papa."

But when a uniformed Oskar Henkel knocked on the door, she knew she wouldn't have to wait long to find out.

Oskar smirked as he took in the scene in the foyer. "Judging by your display of emotion, I assume you've heard about von Cramm. Good news *does* travel fast."

Meike's father took a protective step forward. "Who might you be?"

"I am afraid we have not been formally introduced, *Herr* Count." Oskar removed his hat and gloves and handed them to Rainer Schultz, a butler who had been employed by Meike's family in one capacity or another since Meike was a toddler. "I'm Lt. Oskar Henkel of the SS. I was assigned to accompany Meike on her trips abroad until she saw fit to seek to have me reassigned."

Meike's father gave her a questioning look but saved his actual queries for Oskar. "Why are you here?"

"I came to speak to your daughter—and to give her the freedom she so desperately seeks." Oskar turned to Meike. "Is there somewhere we can talk in private?"

"In here."

Doubting the freedom Oskar was offering would come without a catch, Meike led him to the study. He took a seat in one of the armchairs she and her father had recently vacated.

"Changing your travel plans without telling me wasn't a very nice thing to do. Neither was the complaint you lodged against me with my superiors. Were you foolish enough to think either would prove successful?"

Meike had sent telegrams to Nazi headquarters and to the German Tennis Association when she arrived in London. When she had heard nothing in return, she had thought her pleas had fallen on deaf ears. Oskar's presence in her home, however, proved she had been sadly mistaken.

"I did what I did because I wanted my life back. I refuse to apologize for my actions."

"I didn't come here seeking an apology."

"Then, as my father said earlier, why are you here?"

"I came to obtain your signature." Oskar retrieved an official-looking document from his valise and placed it on the table between them. "The only way for you to receive the concessions you've asked for is to swear your allegiance to the National Socialist Party."

"And if I don't?"

His reply made her blood run cold. "Do you want what's happened to von Cramm to happen to you?" He unscrewed a fountain pen and carefully placed it on the document. "Sign this form and you will receive everything you have asked for. If you refuse, chances are your family will never see you again outside of a prison cell. Is that the kind of legacy you want to leave behind?"

Before she left New York City, Meike had wondered if she should continue to fight or give in. After she heard the Nazis' latest ultimatum, the choice was clear.

"Don't trouble yourself with my legacy, Oskar. History will decide it for me."

The muscles in Oskar's jaw crawled as he clenched his teeth. "You are refusing to sign?"

"I am."

He picked up the pen and paper and shoved both into his valise. "I must inform you it is my duty to report your refusal to my superiors."

"Do what you want. And tell your superiors they are free to do to me what they will. Allow me to show you to the door." She escorted him to the foyer. As Friedrich and her parents looked on in astonishment at her defiance, she unceremoniously returned Oskar's hat and gloves. "If you have said all you intend to say, please leave my home so my family and I can have dinner in peace. Have a safe trip back to Berlin."

"You will regret this decision, Miss von Bismarck."

"No, Lt. Henkel," she said as she slammed the door in his face, "I don't think I will."

Chapter Seven

April 1938
Rheinsteifel, Germany

After the baggage handlers placed everyone's luggage on the station platform in an orderly line, Helen reached for one of her suitcases and hefted it without thinking. The resulting pain offered a searing reminder that, though improved, her damaged shoulder had not yet healed. She was used to doing things for herself, not being forced to rely on other people for help. Today, though, she didn't see any other way.

Three weeks after the training mishap that had resulted in her injury, she was finally able to raise her right arm above shoulder level without pain, but she was under strict doctor's orders to exert herself as little as possible and to avoid lifting anything heavier than twenty-five pounds. Each of the six pieces of luggage she was traveling with weighed considerably more than that paltry amount. She let the suitcase fall from her grasp and looked around for a porter.

"May I help you, miss?" one asked in heavily accented English.

"Please."

The porter tipped his cap. "Gerhard Maier at your service, *Fraulein.*"

Helen nodded her thanks. She hadn't spoken to Gerhard before he approached her. How had he known she was American? Did he recognize her from a newsreel detailing one of her tournament victories or did something else give her away?

Some spy I am if I can't even fool a porter at the train station. The Nazis will see me coming from a mile away.

Swifty said she was crazy for making the trip to Rheinsteifel alone, and she was starting to think he might be right. Even though Germany and the United States weren't at war, she felt like she was in enemy territory. Sure, she had the gun Lanier had given her, but she hadn't practiced shooting left-handed. If someone approached her with the intent of doing her harm, how was she supposed to protect herself with only one arm?

But the chance to see Meike and spend time with her was worth the threat to her safety. Lanier thought she could use her visit to Meike's home to get closer to her. So did she, though not for the reasons he might have wanted. She needed to know if what she was feeling for Meike was real. She had always been attracted to her—she probably always would—but something was different now. She didn't just want to sleep with her. She wanted a life with her, though she had no idea how to provide it or how to make it last.

Her relationships, if you could call them that, were typically measured in weeks or months and, more often than not, only hours. With Meike, it was different. With Meike, one hundred years wouldn't be enough.

Meike had left her once because she didn't think she was capable of sustaining a real relationship. What if she still felt the same way? And, even worse, what if she was right? That thought frightened Helen even more than the idea of taking on the Nazis in their own back yard.

"Where would you like me to take these?" Gerhard asked after he loaded her bags on a luggage cart.

"Good question."

One for which she didn't have an answer. Meike's telegram said there would be a car and driver waiting to pick her up from the station, but Meike hadn't bothered to mention the make or model of the car or describe its driver. Details that would have come in handy as Helen tried to find her bearings in a country she had visited on several prior occasions but felt abjectly foreign to her on this trip.

She shuddered as she remembered the pro-Nazi and anti-Jewish propaganda that had assaulted her in Munich when the train made a brief stop there before continuing on to its terminus in Rheinsteifel. The swastika flew over the station in Rheinsteifel, too, but things felt different here. Helen felt like she was not only visiting another place but another time as well.

When Meike warned her Rheinsteifel was a small town that lacked the trappings a metropolis like Los Angeles or New York City could provide, Helen had expected to see acres and acres of rolling hills and more cows than people. She hadn't expected this.

The town in which she currently found herself seemed like something out of a fairy tale. Helen could picture knights on horseback riding through the cobblestoned streets, which were lined with houses, churches, and monuments that were nearly a thousand years old. Imagining Meike standing on the balcony of the castle on the edge of town like a princess surveying her kingdom, she wondered if the brothers Grimm had spent time in Rheinsteifel while they wrote some of their famous tales.

"Rapunzel, Rapunzel, let down your hair," she said before the sight of a quartet of khaki-clad Hitler Youth chasing each other down the street brought her fairy tale-fueled fantasy to an abrupt end.

"Pardon me, *Fraulein*," Gerhard said, "but I think the gentleman over there might be looking for you."

Following Gerhard's line of sight, Helen spotted a short, middle-aged man wearing a chauffeur's uniform. The handwritten sign he was holding up bore her name. "You are Helen Wheeler?" the man asked in halting English after she took a few steps in his direction.

"The one and only. Did Meike send you?"

The chauffeur's soft brown eyes crinkled as he flashed a smile tinged with fondness for the subject at hand. "Miss von Bismarck, yes. My name is Rainer. Rainer Schultz. You will come with me, please?"

He bowed and indicated the stately Opel Olympia parked by the curb. The car's name reminded Helen of the 1936 Olympics, when American track star Jesse Owens had embarrassed Adolf Hitler in his own backyard by singlehandedly disproving the German leader's claims of Aryan superiority. The four gold medals Jesse had taken home from Berlin had earned him the moniker of hero. Helen doubted her mission would garner similar accolades for her. Considering the veil of secrecy she was under, headlines were out of the question and she might not receive much more than a "thank you." Provided, of course, she was able to pull off what she had been assigned to do. Basic training was over. She had finally made it to the front lines. But did she have what it took to see her task through to the end?

She climbed into the backseat of the Opel as Rainer stored her luggage in the spacious trunk. Then she sat back and enjoyed an impromptu tour as Rainer pointed out the main attractions. By far, the tallest, most imposing building in the town filled with squat, orange-roofed houses was the medieval castle Meike called home.

At the train station, Helen had admired Meike's childhood home from a distance. Up close, the structure took her breath away. The shingles on the conical towers on each corner were obviously new, but the limestone in the rest of the abode appeared to be original. Some of the huge blocks bore scars from past assaults by man, Mother Nature, or both. Helen craned her neck to see the towering keep and the battlements that now served as a widow's walk.

"Impressive, isn't it?" Meike asked.

"That's one word for it." Helen tore her eyes away from Castle von Bismarck and rested them on something even more beautiful: Meike's smiling face. The tension she had observed in Meike's demeanor the last time they had seen each other was gone now. Meike looked calm. Relaxed. Happy. Here, she didn't have the weight of the world on her shoulders. Here, she didn't have to fear anyone or anything. Here, she was home. "No wonder people call you the Countess. You live like royalty."

"Purely an accident of birth, I assure you." Meike bounded down the steps and gave Helen a crushing hug. Helen winced at the flare of pain in her right shoulder as she tried and failed to return the affectionate gesture.

"If you think this place is something, you should see my cousin's," Meike said after she let go. "It's twice as large and perched on top of the limestone cliff from which it was formed."

"It sounds impregnable."

"One would think so, but, according to family history, it has been ransacked by everyone from the Gauls to the Saxons to the Huns. Rainer, please take Miss Wheeler's things upstairs."

"Of course, Miss von Bismarck."

"I have taken the liberty of giving you the room across from me, Helen. My brother's room is down the hall, but it stands empty at the moment since he is away at university."

"Sounds cozy. I hope you plan on joining me from time to time in case I get lonely or afraid of the dark."

Helen's innuendo-laden comment brought color to Meike's cheeks but failed to elicit an acceptance of her invitation.

"I thought you came here to relax."

"I can't think of a better possible way to relax than making love, can you?"

Meike dipped her head and brought her lips so close to Helen's ear Helen could feel her breath brush her skin. "If you found making love to me relaxing, I must have been doing something wrong."

"Give me a refresher course and I'll let you know." Helen nuzzled Meike's cheek, rejoicing in the remembered warmth of her skin. "A girl from Cannery Row and a countess-in-waiting from Germany. That would be the ultimate fairy tale."

But she didn't see a way for this fairy tale to have a happy ending. Not when she was living the ultimate irony: lying in an attempt to uncover the truth.

Meike's father cleared his throat to announce his presence. "I'm not interrupting anything, am I?"

"Of course not, Papa." Meike took Helen's uninjured arm and led her up the steps. "You remember my father, don't you?"

"Certainly. It's a pleasure to see you again, Count von Bismarck."

"The pleasure is mine," he said as he bent to kiss the back of Helen's hand. "And, please. It's Max, remember?"

"Yes. How could I forget?"

Helen had never met Meike's mother, but she had been introduced to Maximilian von Bismarck, Meike's father, a few years earlier. He had treated Helen and Meike to dinner after a tournament in Hamburg to celebrate their victory in the doubles final. Max had proven to be a witty and charming dinner companion, but he had been filled with so many questions about her game Helen had felt like she was being interviewed.

"And this," Meike said, indicating the woman to Max's left, "is my mother, Katharina."

"Countess." Katharina looked so regal, Helen had to fight the urge to curtsy. She settled for a handshake instead.

"Please call me Katja. Welcome to our humble home."

"I hope I'm not imposing."

Katja gave Helen's hand a reassuring pat. "When it comes to overnight visitors, I'm normally an ardent proponent of Benjamin Franklin's quote about fish and houseguests stinking after three days. But for you, my dear, I will gladly make an exception. My husband is an ardent fan, and my daughter has sung your praises for years. It is a pleasure to finally make your acquaintance. The news of your impending arrival has managed to shake the gloom that had descended upon us after we received word of Gottfried von Cramm's arrest, followed by Meike's decision to force Friedrich into exile."

Meike sighed as if the argument she and her mother were about to have was an old one. "I didn't force Friedrich into anything, Mother, and, in your heart, you know leaving was the right thing for him to do. He resisted the notion at first, but in the end, remaining in France long enough to secure safe passage to Switzerland was a decision he made."

"After following your advice. It is my fear that Friedrich's very public defection will cause the Nazis to double their efforts against you. I don't want saving a friend's life to cost you your own."

"Neither do I, but I'm doing what needs to be done."

"Doing or have done?" Meike's silence gave Katja the answer she needed—and the one she didn't want. "Please tell me you aren't continuing to help him, Meike. Do you know how dangerous that is? Consider the consequences if you were to get caught smuggling money out of the country."

"I have considered the consequences."

"And you are still willing to take the risk?"

"They can only kill me once," Meike said firmly.

"But, my darling girl, I would die a thousand deaths without you."

"You won't have to."

"Promise me."

Katja held Meike's face in her hands, a moment so tender Helen was forced to look away. She felt like an intruder. An enemy invader. She felt like what she was: someone who didn't belong here.

"I promise."

Helen had never known Meike to lie. Until now. She could tell by Meike's expression she had just made a promise they all knew she might not be able to keep.

"Come, Helen." Meike extended her hand. "Let me show you to your room. Then, if you aren't too tired from your long journey, I shall take you on a tour of the house and grounds. This place has dozens of rooms. Unless you plan on leaving a trail of bread crumbs behind you, you won't be able to find your way."

"I'll be fine as long as the path leads me back to you."

The words tumbled out before Helen could stop them. The beaming smile on Meike's face made her wish she had said them sooner.

"No wonder my father finds you so charming."

"What about you? How do you find me?"

"Irresistible. That's my second-favorite English word."

"What's your first?"

"Yes."

Helen drew a fingertip across Meike's palm, eliciting a shiver. "I can't wait to hear you say your favorite English word, preferably at the top of your lungs."

"No. I brought you here to rest. I won't be responsible for setbacks in your recovery. Tennis wouldn't be the same without you on the court."

And my life, Helen thought, hasn't been the same without you in my bed.

Two winding staircases led to the second floor. One pointed to the east wing of the castle, the other to the west. The room Meike showed her to was bigger than some apartments Helen had rented over the years. A large four-poster bed sat in the middle of the room. An oak dresser, chest of drawers, and wardrobe large enough to stand in offered more than ample storage room for her clothes, which two maids had already started to unpack and put away.

Thankful she had hidden the gun in her purse instead of one of her suitcases, she tightened her grip on her handbag's leather strap. She deposited the purse in the nightstand after the maids took their leave. Here, the only thing that needed protection was her heart. And a gun wouldn't do the trick.

"When were you going to tell me about Friedrich? When the Nazis came to drag you away for helping him escape?"

Meike seemed disappointed by the conversational shift. Helen would have preferred flirting, too, but she couldn't ignore the very serious subject at hand.

"What is there to tell?" Meike asked. "He is with Hans and they are both safe. That is all that matters."

"Your mother made it sound like there's considerably more to the story. I don't mean any disrespect, but I choose to believe her version of events rather than yours."

"My mother has a tendency to exaggerate upon occasion."

"Meike, I heard the fear in her voice."

"All mothers worry, Helen. In that respect, mine is no different from anyone else's."

Helen wasn't willing to take the situation as lightly as Meike seemed to be. "Your mother is afraid for you. Should I be?"

Meike looked away. "Don't make me lie to you, Helen."

Helen forced Meike to face her. "Then tell me the truth."

Meike looked at her, unblinking. "You first."

Helen could feel her palms start to sweat. She pulled away, praying Meike hadn't noticed. Or guessed the real reason she was here. "What do you want to know?"

"How you hurt your arm and why you reached out to me for help when you have friends and quite a few lovers who are thousands of miles closer to you than I am."

"Distance is my least favorite method of measuring closeness. For friends or lovers." Helen pushed a lock of hair behind Meike's ear and held it there. "I feel closer to you than anyone in my life. I always have. I probably always will."

"Why?"

Helen considered the question. "Because you are the first— no, the *only* woman I've ever loved."

Meike looked torn between moving closer and moving away. Unfortunately, she chose the latter. "I don't need or want you to love me, Helen, so please don't say those words to me ever again."

Meike headed for the door, but Helen's voice stopped her before she reached it.

"Why? Because you're too afraid to repeat them to me? To admit you still have feelings for me? I know you loved me, Meike. I could feel it every time you kissed me. I could see it every time you looked at me. I could hear it every time you called my name. Nothing has changed between us. You still want me as much as I want you. I know you do. I couldn't give you what you wanted then, but I can now if you just stop running away. How can someone who's brave enough to defy the Nazis be such a coward when it comes to following her heart?"

Meike whirled around, her eyes blazing white-hot. When she spoke, her words were just as heated.

"You're right. Nothing has changed between us. You know why? Because we haven't changed. I still want what I've always wanted and so do you. This isn't a game, Helen. It's my life. So stop trying to tell me what you think I want to hear instead of what you really feel. On the *Southern Star*, you asked me why I ended things with you. I left before you grew bored and decided to cast me aside like you did that awful woman who insulted me at the Cotton Club."

"I would never have walked away from—"

"Of course you would. Because that is what you do. I have seen you do it time and time again, and I didn't want you to do it to me. I didn't leave because I didn't love you, Helen. I left because I did. Sometimes, it takes more courage to walk away from what you love than to hold it close. Hopefully, you will never have to make that choice."

❖

Needing to regain her composure before she lost complete control of it, Meike crossed the hall and retreated to the safety of her room. She closed the door behind her, then leaned against it to keep from sinking to the floor.

Inviting Helen to come to Germany was a mistake. Having Helen here in her home was a mistake. She was tempting fate by bringing Helen so close to danger. Tempting fate by bringing Helen so close to her. She felt foolish for thinking she could keep her feelings for Helen at bay and for, however briefly, considering giving in to them once more.

She had decided years ago that nothing could come of a relationship with Helen. Why was she second-guessing herself now? Because that mistake might have been the biggest of all.

She should have kept Helen at a distance. For Helen's sake as well as her own. If she had done that, she wouldn't be in this position: regretting what once was and mourning what could never be.

Helen's visit had barely begun and Meike was already wondering when it would end. What had she been thinking? That was the problem. She hadn't been thinking. She had been feeling. Something that, despite her family's riches, she couldn't afford to do.

Logic said she couldn't give in to emotion. Logic said she had to be impervious to her feelings. Hurt. Pain. Fear. And, most of all, love. But logic also said it was easier to give in to the Nazis than to fight them. How could using logic be right on one hand if it was so wrong on the other? Because nothing about love was logical. And, like it or not, she was in love with Helen Wheeler.

Someone knocked on the door. Tentatively. Uncertainly. Meike opened the door feeling the same way. Helen stood on the other side, freshened up from her long train trip from Paris and bearing no lasting effects of the argument they had gotten into a few minutes before.

Meike used to be able to compartmentalize her feelings like that. To forgive and forget at a moment's notice. Now she couldn't do either. All she could do was remember. How she and Helen used to be. How she wished they could be once more. How they could never be again.

"Hey, champ. How about that tour you promised me?"

Helen's smile was sincere, inviting, and utterly irresistible. It made Meike feel like everything she had once thought impossible was now within reach. Yet why did it still seem so unattainable?

"Where do you want to start?" she asked.

"Wherever you take me."

Helen held out her hand. Meike took it, unsure of where the journey might lead but certain she wanted to make it with Helen. She showed her the main rooms on the first and second floors and taught her how to navigate from them to her room. Then she took her up to the keep, the fortified tower that afforded visitors brave enough to climb its winding steps dazzling views of the lush green inner courtyard as well as the tranquil waters of Lake Bodensee.

"Where are the hidden passageways?" Helen asked. "Every castle I've ever read about has at least one."

"We have several. One is in my room and one is in my parents' room, but the most spacious by far is in the den. There is a secret lever built into the bookcase. I will show you where it is when we go back inside. My brother and I used to hide in the passageways when we were children. It was great fun listening to the search parties calling our names as they looked for us. Then my parents ruined it all by learning to exercise patience. They figured out if they waited long enough, hunger would win out over our impishness and Michael and I would eventually come out of hiding. The passageways were fun, but the keep was always my favorite part of the house. Michael and I would come up here all the time. We would pretend to be knights in shining armor defending the castle from enemy invaders. Our dog, Hildegard, was the damsel in distress."

"Hildegard? You mean the lump of hair we saw lounging by the fire?"

Meike pretended to take offense. "Hilde has earned the right to be a woman of leisure. In her youth, she was a beautiful princess."

"Should I start calling you Sir Galahad instead of Countess?"

Meike chuckled. "Champ will do."

Some might see the term as a nod to her accomplishments, but she preferred to view it as a sign of respect. Knowing she had earned Helen's respect meant a great deal to her. Only earning her love could mean more. But the time for that had come and gone, no matter how hard Helen tried to convince her otherwise. She wanted to believe Helen meant what she said—desperately so—but what could come of it if she did? Nothing but more heartache. For both of them.

She pointed to the castle. "It's easy to get disoriented, but we came from that way. That's the east wing, where our rooms are. My parents live over there in the west wing. Guests, when we have them, end up scattered somewhere in between."

Helen turned in a slow circle to get her bearings. She regarded the keep, the courtyard, and the rectangular castle that surrounded both. "What about the servants? Do they live in the attic or the dungeon?"

"Neither," Meike said with a laugh. "Except for Rainer, they all have houses in town."

"Where does he stay?"

"He has a room on the first floor. Down there, near the base of the keep. He moved in after his wife, Leni, died a few years ago. He and Leni had no children. He was lost without her. To be honest, I think my family and I would be lost without him as well."

"How long has he been with you?"

"Over fifty years. He started working here when he was a boy of fifteen. My father's parents were in charge of the estate then. A few years after my parents got married, my grandparents decided to hand over control of the estate to them. My grandparents moved to our summer home in the south of France, where they still live."

"Ah, so that's why you play the tournament in St. Tropez each year. I thought it was the stunning view of all those topless women on the beach."

"Not quite." Meike laughed again, something she always seemed to do when Helen was around. Whether she wanted to or not. "When my grandparents left for France, they assumed Rainer would go with them, but his devotion to this house and these grounds is so complete, he couldn't bear to be separated from them. My father tells the story a bit differently, though. He says Rainer's loyalty isn't to the property but to me. Papa says he couldn't tell who was prouder when I was born, himself or Rainer."

"Rainer would do anything for you, wouldn't he?"

Meike felt her cheeks warm. "Not just me. My brother, too. Rainer is quite fond of Michael as well."

"But I bet he wouldn't help Michael take on the Nazis."

"What do you mean?" Meike stiffened, fearing she might have put a lifelong friend in danger. Then she forced herself to relax. This wasn't someone looking to denounce her or her family in order to improve their own chances of survival. This was Helen. This was someone she could trust. With some things. Her heart was still off-limits.

"Smuggling money to Friedrich and getting away with it isn't something you could do on your own. You have to have help. A courier. A distraction. A decoy. Something. Does Rainer help you?"

Meike smiled at how close Helen had come to guessing the truth. "I am sure he would if I asked, but I would never ask him or anyone I loved to put their lives at risk. I would only risk my own."

"You wouldn't have to ask. If you needed his help, I'm sure Rainer would volunteer. So would I."

"You wouldn't say that if you knew the consequences."

"If you get caught, you could be sent to prison and sentenced to hard labor, you could end up in a concentration camp, or you could die. I know the risks, Meike, but if you're willing to take them, so am I. Friedrich's my friend, too. I want to help you. Both of you." Helen gripped Meike's arm. Meike could feel passion as well as sincerity in her touch. "Now tell me how you do it."

Meike plunged ahead, diving headfirst instead of sticking in a toe to test the waters. "There is a passageway I haven't told you about. A tunnel that is dank and dark and not very much fun. It is a little over ten kilometers long and just tall and wide enough for an average-sized man to walk through without having to stoop."

"A six mile-long tunnel? Where does it lead?"

Meike stared into the distance. Toward the invisible border that separated Germany from Switzerland.

Helen's eyes widened in recognition. "So that's how you manage to make the trip undetected. But isn't it dangerous? A tunnel that old could collapse at any time."

"Over the years, my family has shored up the areas that need the most support, but, hopefully, I won't need to make many more trips through it. A friend at Friedrich's bank helped liquidate his accounts before we left for France a few weeks ago. He has nearly all the funds now. There are only a few thousand marks left to forward him."

"Don't you usually play in Lausanne a few weeks after the French Championships? Why can't you pass off the money then instead of risking another trip through the tunnel?"

"Because Lausanne is too public. The only place I have any semblance of privacy is here. When I leave Rheinsteifel, I can't go anywhere without someone trailing me. I have been put, as you Americans say, on a very short leash."

"Who's holding the end of the harness," Helen asked contemptuously, "Oskar Henkel?"

"If not him, then someone like him. In the end, they are all interchangeable."

Helen shook her head in wonder. "How do you do it? How do you play and win with all this pressure on your shoulders?"

"Because I have no choice."

"We all have a choice, Meike. Some easy, some difficult. You simply have to make the one that's best for you."

The time to make a choice was coming. When it arrived, Meike knew the decision would be much harder than Helen made it seem. For her sake, she hoped she would make the right one.

Chapter Eight

May 1938
Rheinsteifel, Germany

Helen leaned over and flipped on the radio sitting on the nightstand. Hearing Adolf Hitler's voice blaring from the speakers instead of the detective shows she favored took some getting used to. So did seeing the German people react to what was happening in their country. The newsreels she had watched back in the States made it seem like all Germans unanimously supported their leader and there were no dissenting voices. Now that she was here, she knew that wasn't the case. Yes, the Nazis had more than their fair share of followers, but they had just as many enemies, too. Not only people in positions of power, but ordinary citizens like the ones in Rheinsteifel. The tiny town's residents visibly stiffened when news of another atrocity broke and couldn't meet their neighbors' eyes whenever Hitler's voice came over the radio like it did now.

Helen changed the station before Hitler got too warmed up, but the damage had already been done. Barbara, the maid who had been chatting amiably as she tidied the room, fell silent. Then her face went pale and her body language became as tense as Meike's did whenever Helen asked her to weigh in on the worsening political situation in the country of which she was once so proud.

Barbara's movements became jerky as she tried to complete her assigned tasks and make herself invisible at the same time. In her haste to escape Helen's scrutiny, she accidentally knocked over a pitcher of water. "I am sorry, Miss Wheeler. Please forgive me."

"No need to apologize." Helen switched the radio to a Swiss station playing French-language love songs. The pleading in the lovelorn singer's voice seemed to make Barbara more uncomfortable instead of less. In fact, she seemed on the verge of tears as she dabbed at the damp carpet with a cleaning cloth. "Relax. It's water, not red wine. I don't think it will leave a stain."

"Yes, Miss Wheeler. I mean, no, Miss Wheeler. I mean—"

Helen held up her hands. "It's okay. I'm one of the good guys."

Barbara was only in her early twenties, but her eyes made her seem twice that age. She looked at Helen as if she had heard the "good guy" line before and wasn't going to allow herself to be fooled a second time. "Yes, Miss Wheeler."

After Barbara gathered her cleaning supplies and scurried out of the room, Helen tried to decide whether she should include the incident in the report she was writing for Paul Lanier. Even though she didn't consider what had happened a big deal, Uncle Sam might. After she added the additional details, she set the report aside until she could seal it in an envelope and take it to the post office in the village. Just as she did every week.

Her trips into the town center weren't unusual. To stay in shape, she and Meike took long walks through the streets of Rheinsteifel twice a day. Meike showed her the sights and introduced her to everyone they met along the way. In the mornings, they would stop by Meike's favorite bakery for a pastry and a cup of coffee. In the early evening, they would return to town for a stein of beer and a plate of braised pork leg or a bowl of hearty stew. When they made it back to the castle, Almuth would have a meal waiting to satisfy the appetites they had worked up during the walk home. Helen had never eaten so much or so well in her life.

But the food wasn't the best part. The best part was seeing Meike in her element. Seeing her be truly, completely herself. Everyone they passed on the street or encountered in a restaurant greeted Meike by name. They knew her not because she was an internationally famous athlete but because she had grown up here. They knew her because she was one of them.

Helen had never received such universal approval. In her family's eyes, she was a cause for shame rather than pride. They made their disapproval of her lesbianism loud and clear. They weren't fond of her athletic ability, either. Her gifts, she was told time and time again, were wasted on her and would have done more good if they had been given to one of her brothers instead. But Mrs. Johnson, her first supporter and most ardent fan, hadn't seen it that way. Neither did the villagers in Rheinsteifel.

The people here didn't make her feel like an outsider. From the watchmaker she had drunk under the table to the butcher who kept trying to convince her that her shoulder would heal faster if she ate more red meat, they made her feel like she belonged. She knew her time here couldn't last, but she wasn't ready for it to come to an end. Perhaps she could find a way to extend it indefinitely. The next forty or fifty years would be a good start. If Meike would have her. And that scenario seemed highly unlikely given Meike's reluctance to give her a second chance. Or was it a third? At this point, she had lost count.

Meike knocked on the door and stuck her head inside. "Are you ready?"

"Almost. Let me get my coat." Helen's stomach growled in anticipation of yet another fabulous meal while her heart soared at the thought of spending more time with Meike. She placed a book over the report she was writing and climbed off the bed. Then she grabbed her coat and shrugged it on. "Where are we off to tonight, the place with the great currywurst or the one that brews its own beer?"

"Neither. Tonight, I have something a little different in mind."

"How different?"

"You'll see." Meike tied a black kerchief around her head, covering her hair. Paired with a dark brown trench coat, the kerchief made her look almost dowdy. Far from the glamorous figure Helen was used to seeing. "What are you working on so diligently?"

Helen felt a surge of panic when Meike lifted the book and reached for the handwritten pages underneath the leather-bound tome. "Nothing important." She plucked the pages from Meike's hands before Meike had a chance to see her name written on them.

"If it isn't important, why won't you let me see it?"

Meike reached for the pages, but Helen switched them from one hand to the other, then hid them behind her back. "What I've written would only bore you to tears."

"Now I truly am curious."

Meike took another swipe at the pages, but Helen brought the impromptu game of keep-away to an abrupt end. "If you must know," she said, stashing the report in her coat pocket, "I'm writing a tennis column for one of the LA papers."

Meike's smile slowly faded. "But we're amateurs, Helen. We aren't allowed to make money from tennis-related activities. Bill Tilden has gotten into trouble on multiple occasions for doing something similar. Do you want to get suspended or barred from amateur competition like he did?"

"No, but I don't want to starve to death, either. I can't take appearance fees if I'm not playing, and I can't take a no-show job if everyone knows I'm not physically able to work. I've got to make money somehow. I have bills to pay."

Meike's expression softened. "I understand your dilemma, but you have to be careful, Helen."

"I could say the same to you." Helen was touched by Meike's obvious concern for her well-being. Which made her feel even worse about bending the truth. "The consequences if I get caught writing a column under a pen name pale in comparison to what could happen to you if you get caught helping Friedrich."

"I won't get caught."

"I can't tell who you're trying harder to convince, me or yourself. You've always done a swell job of proving how independent you are. You want everyone to think you don't need anyone to help you with anything and that the only person you need is yourself. But I know better. Everyone needs someone sometime. I needed you to help me take my mind off things after I got hurt. Whether you like it or not, you need me, too. Let me help you, Meike."

"You can't possibly comprehend what you're asking, Helen."

"Yes, I do. I'm asking you to trust me. I know trusting someone is a decision you don't take lightly, but if you take a chance on me, you can rest assured I won't let you down."

Meike's expression was inscrutable, but her eyes twinkled with amusement. "Now who is the one trying to do the convincing?"

Helen grinned. "Did it work?"

Meike regarded her for so long Helen began to wonder if her attempted joke had fallen flat. Finally, Meike said with an enchanting tilt of her head, "How would you like to take a longer walk than usual tonight?"

"I'm in the mood for dinner, not exercise. How far is the new restaurant you have in mind?"

"Six miles. One way, that is." Meike patted the pockets of her coat. "I have bread and sausages in case we get hungry along the way."

Helen was rendered momentarily speechless by the import of Meike's request. Meike wasn't taking her to dinner. She was asking her to take part in an activity she kept secret from everyone else. "Did you plan to ask me to accompany you tonight even before you came in here?"

Meike cupped her hand against Helen's cheek. "Perhaps."

By earning Meike's trust, Helen had fulfilled her mission. She felt relieved that one part of her job was done, but the hardest part was yet to come: betraying what she had worked so hard to gain.

"Let's take a walk." In case they found themselves in a situation they couldn't talk their way out of, she pulled her pistol from its hiding place and slipped it into her pocket while Meike's back was turned. Then she followed Meike across the hall.

In her bedroom, Meike placed her hand on a stone that looked just like all the others. But when she exerted pressure on the stone, a panel next to the fireplace opened inward and a blast of cold air rushed into the room. She pulled a flashlight from her pocket and shined the beam into the passageway. "This way."

Helen recoiled from the damp, musty smell that assaulted her senses, but, convinced Meike wouldn't lead her astray, stepped into the unknown.

❖

Meike tore off a chunk of bread and unwrapped one of the sausages. "Care to trade?"

Helen exchanged the flashlight Meike had asked her to hold for the wax paper-wrapped bundle of food. "How far do you think we've gone?" she asked between bites.

Meike shined the flashlight on her watch. She and Helen had been in the tunnel for almost ninety minutes and, provided they kept up the same steady pace, had about another half hour to go before they reached the other side. "Nearly five miles."

"We're almost there." Helen wolfed down the rest of her sandwich and shoved her hands in the pockets of her overcoat. "And not a minute too soon. I don't know which is worse, the cold or the tight space."

Meike played the flashlight beam over the walls of the tunnel. Cobwebs hung from nearly every available surface. She usually came face-to-face with several each time she made the arduous journey. Tonight was no different. Her kerchief and the shoulders of her coat were so white they seemed to be made of silk.

"The claustrophobia usually disappears after the first few meters. By the time I reach this point, I'm too numb to feel the cold."

"Where do your parents think we are tonight?"

"Visiting friends. I told them we would be very late and not to expect to see us until the morning."

"Do you think they suspect where we are?"

"I would say no, but I'm not willing to bet against my mother's maternal instincts." Meike chuckled. She was normally filled with trepidation when she made this journey. Tonight, she felt uncharacteristically light. She felt stronger having Helen by her side. She felt safe. She hoped to remain that way. She hoped they both would. "Whenever Michael and I hid in the passageways, she always knew exactly where to look."

"I envy the close-knit relationship you have with your parents. In my family, there were so many kids I often felt like an afterthought."

"But I'm sure your parents are proud of your successes."

Helen's disgusted snort echoed off the stone walls. Meike heard a rat, frightened by their presence, scamper past them in search of safer ground.

"My parents aren't as accepting as yours."

"Is that why you don't speak about them?"

Meike had noticed the obvious void in Helen's life, but she had never been able to convince her to discuss it. The subject was just too sore. She wouldn't be where she was without her family's support. She admired Helen for finding success—and maintaining it—on her own.

"One of many reasons. They don't approve of the way I live my life or what I do for a living. As if I had a choice about either. If I had showed them the professional contract that was dangled in front of me a few months ago, things might be different. Seeing all those zeroes would have gotten their attention, that's for sure. It might have even earned their respect."

"If proving yourself to your family is so important to you, why didn't you become a professional when you had the chance?"

Helen hesitated. The moment was brief but obvious. And unexpected. The question was straightforward. The response should have been as well, but when it came, it seemed rehearsed rather than honest, raising more questions than it answered.

"Someone has to bring your winning streak to an end. I want it to be me. I can't do that if we're playing on different circuits."

"Tell me the truth, Helen." Meike wanted to turn around so she could see Helen's face, but the footing was too treacherous for her to be able to take her eyes off the slippery path in front of her and they didn't have time to stop. Not if they wanted to be in their beds before sunrise. Not if they didn't want to get caught. "I was honest with you. Why can't you be the same with me?"

"You don't think I want to beat you?"

"I'm sure you do. Every player worth her salt wants to be able to say she defeated the top-ranked player, but if money is as important to you as you make it seem, defeating me can't be your primary motivation."

"You're right." Her touch as gentle as her voice, Helen placed a hand on Meike's shoulder and compelled her to turn around. "Beating you isn't the reason I decided not to turn pro. But loving you is. That's why I didn't sign the contract. That's why I'm here now risking life and limb in order to keep you safe. Because I love you, Meike."

Meike gasped when Helen's lips met hers. She was surprised by both the coldness of Helen's skin and the warmth of her kiss. As the kiss deepened, Helen backed Meike against the tunnel wall and pressed her body against hers. Instead of pushing Helen away as instinct told her to do, Meike buried a hand in her hair and pulled her closer.

She didn't just want Helen. She needed her, too. More than she had ever needed anyone else. She needed her light to banish the darkness that surrounded her. If only for a little while.

"I love you, too, Helen," she said when their lips finally parted. "God help me, I love you, too."

Helen's hands fumbled at the buttons of Meike's coat. Helen's mouth, hot and wet, latched onto the side of her neck. She explored Meike's mouth with her tongue, taking her breath away.

"This is crazy."

"I know, but I need you, Meike. Now. Forever." She reached under Meike's dress and cupped her sex through the thin silk of her underwear. Meike felt herself grow wet long before she heard Helen's fervent whisper. "Please."

Meike released the flashlight and allowed it to clatter to the ground. The beam played on the tunnel walls as the flashlight rolled away. Meike arched her neck, giving in to desire. Giving in to Helen. "Take me. Now. Forever."

Helen slipped Meike's underwear off and slipped one, then two fingers inside her.

"Yes," Meike hissed as she began to move against Helen's hand.

"Your favorite English word." Meike could feel Helen's lips, pressed against her cheek, curl into a smile. "Say it again."

"Yes. Yes. Oh, God, yes," Meike said as Helen continued to stroke her. She wrapped her arms around Helen's shoulders and held on tight. It had been so long since she had been touched this deeply. So long since she had felt this kind of connection with someone. Others had tried, but only Helen could make her feel this way. Like she was falling. Like she was flying. Like she was part of something bigger than herself.

The tremors started much too soon, beginning low in her belly then branching out until she thought her body would come apart.

"Yes. I think that might be my favorite English word, too." As Meike's breath came in ragged bursts, Helen kissed her again. Gently. Tenderly. But hinting at the passion Meike could feel bubbling just below the surface. Meike wanted to take Helen on the journey she had just traveled, but Helen wouldn't let her. "We'd better get going," Helen said, reminding her of the reason they had entered this dark, dank tunnel. "We don't want to leave Friedrich waiting. But make no mistake. We have unfinished business, you and I."

"Yes?" Meike picked up the flashlight and held it so she could see Helen's face. The face of the woman she loved.

"I want to spend the rest of the night making love to you. Then I want to greet the morning with you in my arms."

Meike swiped at the cobwebs clinging to Helen's curls. "Does a long, hot bath factor into your plans somewhere?"

Helen murmured her assent. "You'd be amazed what I can do with a bar of soap."

Meike drew her in for another kiss. "Are you sure you don't believe in fairy tales?"

"Believe in them? I think I'm living one."

"And, thanks to you, I've found my very own happily ever after."

But how long could it last?

❖

Helen saw a light at the end of the tunnel, a dim glow that grew brighter with each step.

"We're here," Meike said just before her flashlight flickered and died. She reached for the spare battery and swapped it for the old one with practiced ease.

Just as she had for the past two hours, Helen followed in Meike's footsteps. She didn't know what to expect. Who would be waiting for them when they exited the tunnel? Who was holding the light glowing in the distance, friend or foe? Meike had traveled this route without incident several times in the preceding weeks, but this time could be different. This time, they could be walking into a trap.

Meike grew quieter the closer they came to the tunnel's opening, but Helen could hear her anxious breathing. No matter how many times Meike made this subterranean trip, it obviously never got any easier. In fact, it only got more dangerous. Each trip was like a round of Russian roulette. Helen hoped tonight wasn't the night the bullet finally found its way into the chamber. She slipped her hand into her pocket to make sure the gun was still there—and prayed she wouldn't have to use it.

The light in the mouth of the tunnel flashed three times in rapid succession. Meike used her flashlight to respond in kind. "It is safe," she said, the words sounding more like a sigh of relief than a statement of fact.

Meike broke into a run. Helen followed suit. They hustled out of the tunnel and dove into the backseat of a waiting car. Meike lay prone on the leather seat and motioned for Helen to do the same. Helen curled up next to her.

"You didn't tell me you were bringing company," Friedrich said as he covered them with a blanket. "It is good to see you again, Helen." The blanket muffled the sound of his voice and disguised the timber. Helen couldn't tell if he sounded excited or anxious. "Drive faster, Hans. We have much catching up to do and not a great deal of time to do it."

Despite Friedrich's request, Hans drove almost as slowly as Helen and Meike had made their way through the tunnel on foot. The trip through the streets of Rorschach, Switzerland, seemed to take hours before they finally reached their destination.

"Come in." Friedrich opened the car door and ushered them inside a house that would have made Hansel and Gretel proud. The walls weren't made of gingerbread, but the overall effect was just as sweet. "The place is small, but it is ours. And most importantly, there are no SS agents breaking down our doors to take it away from us."

Hans led everyone to the kitchen, where a big pot of potato soup simmered on the wood-burning stove. "Sit. Eat," he said after he and Friedrich greeted them with kisses on their cheeks. "But give me your coats first. I'll try to get them clean as best I can and place them by the fire so they can be nice and warm when you begin your journey home."

Helen eagerly stripped off her soiled coat, washed her hands in the sink, and filled a large earthenware bowl with two ladles of soup. The tunnel's cold had permeated her bones and she desperately needed to get warm. She held the bowl in her hands, inhaled the rising steam, and allowed the warmth to seep into her.

Meike reached inside the lining of her coat and pulled out a bulging envelope. "This is for you, Fritzi."

Friedrich took the envelope from Meike and gave her a hug. "I want to thank you for all you've done for me," he said, his voice breaking, "but the words feel inadequate."

Meike patted his damp cheek. "Words have never been necessary between us. They never will be."

"But I hope you will manage to find them if you ever need my help."

"I will."

Friedrich's eyes gave away his obvious doubts that Meike would ever seek the refuge she had helped him find. Helen had the same concerns. Meike's life was in Germany and her heart was in Rheinsteifel. No matter how bad things got for her at home, Helen didn't think Meike would ever leave.

"Enjoy your meal," Friedrich said. "I'll be back after I put this away for safekeeping."

Meike prepared herself a bowl of soup and took a seat next to Helen. "Do you want to talk about what happened in the tunnel?"

"No." Helen covered Meike's hand with hers. Even though she had meant everything she had said and done in the tunnel, she had only confessed her feelings to keep from blowing her cover. It felt dishonest somehow. She needed to make things right. She needed to apologize. The only way she knew how. "The time for talking is past. I don't want to tell you how I feel about you. I want to show you instead." She leaned over and gave Meike a kiss. "I hope your parents aren't light sleepers. If they are, they might hear us on their side of the house."

"Exactly what do you have in mind?"

"You'll see." Helen was now looking forward to instead of dreading the two-hour return trip through the tunnel. Because when the journey was over, she would get to make love to Meike. Slowly and reverently, not with the desperation she had felt in the tunnel. She had once hoped Meike would never discover what Lanier had asked her to do. If she did uncover the truth, Helen doubted Meike would be able to find it in her heart to forgive her. As long as she played her cards right, she had reasoned, Meike would never know what she'd been up to all these months. And when her job was done, they would both be free. But she could see now that she was wrong for keeping the truth from Meike. If she wanted to be with Meike—and she had never wanted anything or anyone more—she had to be honest. No matter how much it might hurt. "Meike, we need to talk."

Meike slowly dragged her thumb across Helen's lip. "Morning will be here soon. As you said, the time for talking is over. I, too, want to show you how I feel about you."

When Meike placed her hand on Helen's leg and gave it a gentle squeeze, Helen felt desire flow through her like a river. "Do you have any idea how much I want you?"

Meike flashed a coquettish smile. "You can show me when we return to Rheinsteifel."

"How soon can we leave?"

Friedrich laughed as he sat across from them. "I'm so glad to see you looking this happy, Meike. You deserve it."

"What about me?" Helen asked.

"The jury, as they say, is still out."

They laughed at the joke and reminisced for a while about their shared history. Several minutes passed as they told stories that began with "Do you remember the time" and ended in raucous laughter. But the levity ended when Hans came into the room, a troubled expression on his face.

"What is it?" Friedrich rose from his seat so fast his chair tipped and fell over. "What's wrong?"

Helen felt fear—real fear—for the first time since she'd arrived in Europe. The warm welcome she had received from Meike's family and the laughs she had shared with Meike and Friedrich had filled her with a false sense of security. She had thought they were safe here in the warm kitchen of a quaint little house filled with love. But the look on Meike's and Friedrich's faces revealed the truth: in this day and age, no part of the continent was safe.

"Granted, my grasp of English isn't as good as I would like it to be," Hans said hesitantly in German, "but I think I have found some things you should see."

He placed a pistol and several wrinkled sheets of paper on the table. Helen realized with a sinking heart that, while cleaning her coat, Hans had stumbled across the report she had written for Agent Lanier. The report that detailed her surveillance of Meike and her family. The report that uncovered the truth she had hoped to keep hidden. The report that revealed her identity as a spy.

"I brought the gun for protection and the pages are just some ideas I was putting down on paper for my next newspaper column. Nothing to concern yourselves over."

She reached for the pages, but Friedrich grasped them before she could close her fingers around them. His face fell after he read no more than a few sentences. "It doesn't seem like 'nothing' to me." He pursed his lips in disapproval—and what looked like disappointment. "Meike, I think you should read this."

"Don't," Helen said, making one last desperate grab for the report. "Meike, please don't."

Meike pulled the pages out of Helen's reach, then lowered her eyes to read what Helen had written. When Meike looked up again, her eyes were filled with tears. "You were spying on me? On my family?"

"I can explain," Helen said, but she had no clue how to begin.

"You thought I was a Nazi? You thought I was capable of committing the atrocities attributed to those animals?"

"No, I—You don't understand, Meike."

"You're right. I don't understand. I don't understand how you could look me in the face and lie to me. I don't understand how you could take advantage of my family's hospitality the way you have. I don't understand how you could tell me you love me—how you could make love to me—when you're only in my life because you've been ordered to be. In that respect, you're no different than Oskar Henkel." Helen flinched at the all-too-apt comparison. "He was ordered to be in my life, too, but at least he was honest about his feelings for me. With him, I know exactly where I stand. With you, I'm lost."

"I *was* honest about my feelings for you. I'm with you tonight because I want to be, not because of what I was asked to do. That's how it was at the beginning, but it isn't like that anymore." Helen struggled to find the right words to say. The ones that would convince Meike she had been deceitful because she had to be, not because she wanted to be. Eventually, she found not only the right words to say but the only ones. The only words that would make a difference. The only words that mattered. "I love you, Meike." She reached for her, but Meike pulled away. "Darling, please listen to—"

"Stop, Helen. I don't want to hear any more of your lies. I just want you to go."

"Meike, you don't mean that. Just give me a chance to explain."

"There is nothing to explain. You have taken the time to write it in great detail, leaving nothing to the imagination. I commend you on your hidden talent. I had no idea you were such an accomplished author." Meike tossed the report into the fire. Helen watched the pages curl along the edges, then blacken and burst into flame. "Please leave."

"Where do you expect me to go?" Helen asked hollowly. "I'm not even supposed to be here. How am I supposed to get out of the country when there's no record of me entering it in the first place?"

"I don't know and I don't care."

Helen had never heard Meike sound so cold. When Meike had ended their affair two years before, there had been warmth in her voice, a tenderness that had softened the blow. Helen felt none of that warmth now. And the pain she felt was infinitely worse. Because this time she had only herself to blame. "You don't mean that."

"Yes, I do." Meike's voice trembled, but her resolve was firm. "I never want to see you again."

There was no denying the finality Helen heard in Meike's words. She had lost Meike again. This time not just as a lover but as a friend as well.

Her vision clouded by tears, she ran out of the house and stumbled through the city streets in search of what she could never hope to find: her way home.

Chapter Nine

May 1938
Rheinsteifel, Germany

Meike felt numb. And this time it had nothing to do with the cold. Helen had betrayed her. Helen, a woman she had thought she could trust. Helen, a woman who had professed to love her. She had been wrong to trust Helen and even more misguided to think her feelings were genuine. Based on her actions, Helen had felt nothing for her except curiosity and, perhaps, contempt.

She closed the entrance to the secret passageway behind her, shed her damp kerchief and coat, and lit a fire in the fireplace. She stared at her bedroom door while she warmed her hands on the flickering flames. Had Helen made it back to Rheinsteifel safely or was she still wandering the streets of Rorschach looking for the entrance to the tunnel?

"Forget about her." She turned away from the door and poured herself a healthy glass of whiskey. "Her well-being isn't your concern. She doesn't care about you. She never cared about you. She was only pretending in order to protect her cover."

Her anger swelled as she remembered how Helen had invaded her family's home and privacy under the guise of friendship in order to further her cause. In order to spy on her and her supposed Nazi allies.

Helen had asked her more questions over the past few weeks than she had in the entire time they had known each other. Meike had thought Helen was trying to get to know her better. To get closer to her. She had been right about that, though not for the reason she had hoped. Helen had only been interested in gathering information, not crafting a relationship.

"Keep your friends close and your enemies closer," Meike said bitterly.

She winced as the alcohol seared its way down her throat. But the whiskey's burn paled in comparison to the scorching heat she had felt when Helen's lips had met hers in the tunnel. She closed her eyes as she remembered the feverish way Helen had made love to her. With one touch, Helen had torched her soul. Branded her heart. How could something that had felt so real have proven to be so false?

Meike set her empty highball glass down and crossed the hall. She simultaneously dreaded and anticipated the confrontation she was about to have, but she needed answers. And only Helen could provide them.

As the morning sun began to chase away the dawn, Meike knocked lightly on the guest room door and waited for a response. "Helen?" she asked when she didn't hear a reply. She waited another beat, then pushed the door open and tentatively ventured inside. "Helen?"

The bed was freshly made and the trunks and suitcases that had recently littered the floor had disappeared. The room was empty. Meike opened the dresser, cabinet, and closet. Each proved as empty as the last. Helen was gone.

Almuth stuck her head into the open doorway as she paused on her way to the kitchen. Meike's parents were early risers and would be expecting breakfast soon. "May I help you with something, Miss von Bismarck?" Almuth asked as she tightened the strings of the white apron covering her gray uniform.

"I was looking for Miss Wheeler. Have you seen her this morning?"

"No. Barbara said she left hours ago."

"In the middle of the night?" Helen had managed to make it out of Switzerland, but she was still missing. And possibly in danger. Meike told herself she shouldn't care what happened to Helen, especially after everything she had discovered about her the night before, but she couldn't help being concerned. "Do you know where she went?"

"She woke Rainer and asked him to drive her to the train station. He tried to tell her the trains don't run at that time of night and she should wait until morning, but she was rather insistent. You know how Americans are. Always in a rush to get somewhere. I'm sorry you didn't get a chance to say good-bye to her, but I am sure she will be fine. If you don't need anything else, I had better get to work. Your father has requested potato pancakes today and the potatoes aren't going to grate themselves."

"Yes, of course, Almuth. Thank you."

Meike had felt betrayed in Rorschach. In Rheinsteifel, she felt abandoned. And she couldn't tell which was worse. Unsure where to turn, she returned to her bedroom and crawled into bed. Mental and physical fatigue had left her feeling exhausted. She closed her eyes, hoping to get a few hours' rest, but her mother's agonized wail shattered the early morning silence.

Fearing something dreadful had happened to her father or brother, Meike leaped out of bed and threw the door open. "Mother, what is it?" she asked as she ran down the stairs.

"Save yourself, Meike! They have come for you!"

Meike's mother threw her weight against the front door, but Oskar Henkel and three other SS agents wouldn't be denied entrance.

"Pack a bag, Miss von Bismarck," Oskar said. "You're coming with us."

"Let me guess," Meike said. "The *Führer* wants to see me."

Oskar's malicious smile sent a chill down Meike's spine. "Not today. Today, our leader has something else in mind." He snapped his fingers. "Peter, Lukas." Two baby-faced agents stepped forward and saluted. The third guarded the open door, preventing anyone from passing through it. "Go with her. Make sure she doesn't take anything she doesn't need."

"Yes, sir."

"She hasn't done anything wrong." Meike's mother clutched at Oskar's arm. "You can't take her."

"You're probably unaccustomed to having anyone disagree with you, Countess, but the uniform I'm wearing allows me to do anything I want." Oskar roughly shook Meike's mother's hand off his arm and shoved her to the floor.

Meike's father helped her mother to her feet and turned on Oskar. "This is the second time you have come in my house and disrespected my family, Lt. Henkel. I won't have it. Do you hear me? I won't have it."

When Meike's father took a step toward him, Oskar drew his gun and cocked the hammer. "Stop where you are, Count von Bismarck, or I will kill you where you stand. Your daughter is coming with me."

Despite the gun pointed at his head, Meike's father didn't halt his progress. He took another step toward Oskar. "The only way you are taking her is over my dead body."

"As you wish." Oskar's knuckles turned white as he began to squeeze the trigger.

"No!" Meike stepped in before the standoff got out of hand. "Papa, please calm down," she said, trying to sound as reassuring as she could. "Oskar, put the gun away. I will go with you and your men."

"But what if you don't come back?" her mother asked.

Meike glanced at Oskar, but she couldn't tell by his expression if her absence from her family home would be temporary or permanent. She took her parents' hands in hers. "Everything will be fine. You shall see."

"Thank you for finally being reasonable, Miss von Bismarck. For your sake, I hope it isn't too late." Oskar holstered his gun and jerked his head toward the second floor. "You have five minutes to gather your things. Don't keep me waiting."

Peter and Lukas accompanied Meike to her room. They stood guard while she shoved some of her personal belongings and several days' worth of clothes into a suitcase. After she secured the latches on the suitcase, she sat down hard. Should she slip into the secret passageway and attempt to escape through the tunnel or should she go downstairs and face her fate, whatever it might turn out to be? Her options were limited. If she refused to go with Oskar and his men, her parents would be forced to pay the ultimate price.

She picked up her suitcase, went downstairs, and hugged her parents good-bye. She tried to keep her emotions in check as her father sobbed on her shoulder.

"It's okay, Papa," she said, drying his tears. "Please don't cry."

Her mother was slightly more resolute. "Don't worry about what might happen to your father and me as a consequence," she whispered in Meike's ear as she held her tight. "Do whatever you have to do to survive. Your father and I have lived our lives. We want you to be able to live yours."

"Yes, Mother."

Oskar impatiently drummed his fingers against the leather holster strapped to his side. "I hate to interrupt such a touching scene, but we really must be going."

He nodded to Peter and Lukas, who each took Meike by the arm and marched her to the car waiting in the driveway. They directed her to climb in the backseat, then squeezed in next to her. The third agent slid behind the wheel and Oskar joined him in the passenger seat.

"Make yourself comfortable," Oskar said. "We're going for a nice, long drive."

"Where are you taking me?"

"You'll find out when we get there." He turned to look at her. "How long did you think you could defy the regime before we decided to exact punishment?"

"I have no idea. But I will continue to defy you as long as I draw breath."

Oskar shared a look with his fellow agents before turning his gaze back on her. "We will see if you are still singing the same tune in a few hours. I have a hunch you shall soon be more amenable to my requests."

The car headed east toward Munich. Several hours later, the driver maneuvered the car through a set of iron gates emblazoned with the motto "Work will make you free." Gaunt men and women with shaved heads, hollow eyes, and sallow cheeks watched from behind several rows of barbed wire fences as the car slowly drove past them.

"Where are we?" Meike asked.

"Welcome to Dachau," Oskar said almost gleefully.

Meike recognized the name. Dachau was Germany's first concentration camp. Opened on the grounds of an abandoned munitions factory, the camp had initially housed only political prisoners, but its numbers had recently begun to swell with detainees of all types. Meike assumed the prisoners' "crimes" were represented by the various colored symbols that had been sewn to their uniforms.

"What do the colors mean?"

"Political prisoners wear red badges, professional criminals wear green, Jehovah's Witnesses wear violet, emigrants wear blue, homosexuals like you wear the pink triangle, and Jews, of course, wear the yellow star. There are many more designations, but I won't bother to list them. After you get settled in with the rest of your fellow prisoners, you can ask them yourself. Take her to the *Schubraum*."

Peter and Lukas dragged her out of the car and took her to a building that looked like a warehouse. Inside, she was forced to stand in front of a long, rectangular table and hand over her suitcase to a stone-faced guard who immediately began sifting through her belongings. She watched as, one by one, her possessions joined the piles of like items on the floor.

"Remove your jewelry and take off your clothes." Thinking she must have misheard him, Meike didn't move. The guard slapped his palm on the table so hard the sound was louder than a gunshot. "Now!"

Despite the chill in the cavernous room, Meike felt her face warm. The guards leered at her as she removed her clothes and placed them on the table.

"It is a pity such beauty is wasted on a deviant," Oskar said as she stood naked before him.

Meike placed an arm across her breasts and a hand over her pubis in a vain attempt to regain some of her lost dignity. Making love to Helen in a filthy tunnel, she had felt beautiful. Standing in a pristine warehouse with the uncaring eyes of strangers on her, she felt unimaginably dirty.

Oskar turned to one of the few female guards. "Take her to the showers and give her a uniform. One with a pink badge so everyone knows why she belongs here."

"Would you like me to shave her head first?"

"No." Oskar ran his fingers through Meike's hair. Even though he had her life in his hands, she recoiled from his touch. In return, Oskar fisted his hand in her hair to hold her still. "Do I have your attention now?" He tightened his grip when she didn't respond. She felt droplets of blood form on her scalp and gasped from the pain. "There. That's better."

Meike felt hot tears course down her cheeks as her resolve began to waver. She had never felt so helpless or exposed.

"Your few fans in the Reich call you the Ice Princess because you remain so cool under pressure," Oskar said, "but, in the end, I always knew I would melt that ice or shatter it into a million pieces. You are mine now to deal with as I please. I don't intend to stop until you beg me for mercy. Perhaps not even then."

Oskar's eyes were feral and totally devoid of human compassion.

"I wonder what Liesel sees in you."

Oskar turned purple with rage. He released his grip on Meike's hair and backhanded her across the face. She staggered from the blow and nearly went down. "Liesel Becker is too good for someone like you. I never want to hear her name cross your lips again. Do you understand?" Spittle flew from Oskar's lips like Hitler in the middle of a particularly passionate speech. "I said, 'Do you understand?'"

Oskar drove his fist into Meike's belly. She bent over double, gagging from the pain. "Yes," she gasped as the room began to spin, "I understand."

"Good. We shall talk more after the attendants wash the stink of aristocracy off you."

Meike's legs felt leaden as she allowed herself to be herded into a windowless shower. Several long minutes crawled by after the door slammed shut. She trembled in fear as a foul-smelling liquid streamed from the series of shower heads placed above and beside her. Her skin and eyes burned from the assault. Blinded and disoriented, she heard a panel slide open. She blinked until her vision cleared enough to see part of Oskar's face fill a tiny gap in the door.

"The chemicals are to treat prisoners for lice, ticks, fleas, or any other unwanted creatures they might have picked up before their arrival."

Without warning, ice cold water shot through the jets. The high-powered spray felt like knife points as it pricked Meike's skin. She turned this way and that but could find no escape. Her teeth continued to chatter long after the latest affront ended.

Oskar unlocked the door and tossed her a striped uniform identical to the one she had seen the prisoners wearing when she was driven through the gates. "Get dressed and follow me. I will take you to your new home. The accommodations might not be as lavish as you are accustomed to, but I am sure you shall learn to make do in time."

Meike put on the baggy uniform and oversized shoes and followed Oskar to a military-style barracks. The women residing in it were alive but barely. Most of their bodies were so thin she could see the outline of their skeletons beneath their waxy, grime-covered skin.

"That one is yours." Oskar pointed to an empty bunk topped by a straw-filled mattress and thin wool blanket, but no pillow. Then he addressed the room. "Ladies, and I use the term loosely, please welcome our newest worker, Meike von Bismarck, a proud new addition to your detail. Please be sure to make her stay enjoyable, won't you?"

All eyes turned to Meike after Oskar left the room. She felt trapped when she heard the lock slide into place. She struggled to remember what each symbol meant as some of the women began to circle her.

A woman branded as a professional criminal approached her first. "Are you *the* Meike von Bismarck?" Meike nodded and the woman's eyes widened in response. "But you're famous."

A woman who had been arrested for prostitution spat on the ground. "Fame? What is fame? Money and fame might mean something on the outside. In here, they don't count for much. In here, no one is better than anyone else. And no worse, for that matter."

"What did they arrest you for?" the first woman asked.

Meike shrugged. "I don't rightly know. I wasn't charged or subjected to a trial."

"Then why are you here?"

"Don't be stupid, Eszter," the second woman said. "You see the pink triangle on her uniform, don't you? Why else would she be here?" She turned to Meike and gave her a brief once-over. "Is it true? Are you a lesbian?"

Meike nodded again. She expected the woman to lash out at her in some way. She was looked down on in some circles for preferring the company of women. If this was one of them, she could be targeted by the prisoners as well as the guards. To her surprise, the prostitute's eyes were hard but not judgmental as they examined her face.

"Women aren't as willing as men to pay for what they want, but I have been with a few in my time. Some of them were as rich as you, but none were as pretty."

Meike felt a moment of kinship when the woman gave her a conspiratorial wink. Friends, she guessed, were hard to come by here, where most relationships were temporary rather than long-term, but she couldn't imagine a more valuable commodity.

"My name is Anna. I moved to Germany from Austria six years ago looking for a better life. If I had known I would end up here, I would have stayed in Vienna." Anna poked a grubby finger at her bony chest. "Stick with me. I will show you the ropes. I will let you know which guards are open to accepting bribes and which ones should be avoided at all costs. Sophie, the girl who had this bunk before you, didn't listen when I tried to tell her these things. She thought she could smile pretty and flash her legs to get what she wanted, but some of the guards aren't interested in sex. They don't want to fuck. All they want is to inflict pain and make people suffer."

Meike shuddered at the thought of having to spend the rest of her life in a place where cruelty was more common than kindness.

"Do you have someone waiting for you on the outside?" Anna asked.

"I thought I did." Meike thought of Helen and all the false promises she had made—all the lies she had told—while she was pretending to have feelings for her in order to spy on her. "But there's just my family."

"What I wouldn't give to be able to say the same," Anna said wistfully. She shook her head as if trying to ward off a bad memory. "We will have plenty of time to talk in the days to come. It is late and morning comes early around here. Try to get some sleep."

Meike reluctantly crawled into her lice-infested bunk. The blessed darkness of sleep overtook her almost as soon as she closed her eyes. She was roused several hours later by a pair of rough hands shaking her by her shoulders.

"Rise and shine," Anna said. "You don't want to be late for roll call. If you are, no one gets breakfast. Granted, the shit they call food isn't much, but it is better than nothing. When was the last time you tried working on an empty stomach?" She laughed, flashing blackened teeth sticking haphazardly out of receding gums. "I forgot who I was talking to for a moment. You've probably never worked a day in your life, have you?"

Meike didn't try to deny the obvious.

"Well, you're about to make up for it now."

"What work is done here?" Meike followed Anna to a hard-packed patch of earth where the rest of the women from their barracks had already gathered.

"We make weapons of war for a government that would rather see us dead," Anna said as they joined the orderly line. "Women's fingers, we are told, are the perfect size for making munitions. I used to try to sabotage as much ammo as I could. When the guards started testing the product before they shipped it out, they punished me for it." When Anna held up her work-roughened hands, Meike noticed the tip of the third finger on her left hand was missing. "Good thing I'm not planning on getting married any time soon."

Anna let out an earthy laugh so infectious Meike couldn't help but join her.

"Quiet," Oskar yelled from his perch on the steps of the administration building. "No talking in the line."

"Remember the guards I said you should avoid?" Anna asked in a whisper. "Put that one at the top of your list. He isn't assigned here. He only comes to escort special prisoners like you. But each time he pays us a visit, someone ends up dead. Don't cross him or you could be his next victim."

Meike rubbed the painful bruise on her belly. "I feel like I already am."

The female guard who had escorted her to the shower the day before began reading names from a clipboard in her hands. Each prisoner yelled, "Present," when she heard her name called. Meike remembered performing the same chore each morning in school, but without the armed guards.

After roll call was complete, each woman was handed a chunk of moldy bread and a bowl filled with a ladle of thin gruel crawling with maggots. The other women eagerly dipped the bread into the gruel and began shoveling the foul concoction into their mouths, but Meike balked.

"Eat," Anna urged her, "or you won't have the energy to last a day. Each of us has a quota to fulfill. You won't be any different."

"What happens if I don't meet the quota?"

Anna wiggled her shortened finger. "This is just the beginning."

Meike dipped her bread into the bowl and scooped some of the gruel into her mouth. She gagged when she felt a maggot squirming against the back of her throat, but she forced herself to swallow.

Oskar smiled as he watched her continued degradation. His leather boots gleamed in the sun as he walked toward her and Anna. "How the mighty have fallen." His voice dripped scorn as he walked a slow circle around them. "You have made a new friend, I see. Friends are good to have. You will need plenty of them if you hope to survive your incarceration."

Meike grew dizzy as she tried to track his progress without turning her head.

"Friedrich Stern, the Jew who prefers to dress in women's clothes. He was your friend, too, wasn't he?" Oskar asked rhetorically. "You used the considerable resources at your command to help him escape without leaving the required ninety percent of his assets behind."

Meike felt herself begin to tremble. The harder she tried to stop, the worse the tremors became.

"You have proven you are willing to do anything for your friends. And now you have made friends with this whore. What am I to do? The answer is obvious," he said without waiting for her to respond. "I must save you from further temptation."

Meike's stomach churned as she heard him pull his gun from its holster and cock the hammer. Her shaky resolve broke as he pressed the barrel of the gun to the back of her head. Her bowels released and tears ran down her cheeks. "Please, don't shoot," she begged. "I don't want to die."

"As you wish." Oskar moved the gun from her head to Anna's and pulled the trigger. Meike screamed as bone, blood, and gobbets of something gray splashed the side of her face. Anna's lifeless body slumped to the ground, her open eyes staring sightlessly at the sky. Oskar holstered the smoking gun. "Unless you want to join your newfound friend, I suggest you follow me."

As two prisoners carried Anna's body to a large, open-air pit, tossed it inside, and covered it with lye, Meike trailed Oskar past a series of offices occupied by various SS officials. He entered a room marked as the office of the Gestapo trial commissioner and took a seat behind the desk. No other chairs were available so Meike remained standing.

"It is common knowledge you assisted Friedrich Stern in defecting to Switzerland. Though I cannot prove it, I suspect you have helped smuggle money to him as well." Oskar folded his hands on the desk and regarded her in silence for a few minutes before he resumed speaking. "Effective today, you are no longer allowed to travel to Switzerland for business or pleasure. In addition, you are barred from competing in any tennis tournament outside Europe, which means you will not be allowed to travel to New York to participate in the United States Championships. Unfortunate, considering you had put yourself in position to win the Grand Slam this year, but you brought this upon yourself."

Meike was too stunned to protest. Stunned by Anna's senseless death, Oskar's pronouncement, and the ramifications of both. Even though she wouldn't be able to fulfill a lifelong dream, she would be allowed to leave this place. She would be allowed to live.

"After you compete in the French Championships, you will remain in Paris to participate in the Confederation Cup. You and Liesel will each play singles and you will combine to play doubles. An alternate to be named later will be available in case of injury. The Americans have a formidable team. The Australians, too. But if you commit yourself to the task and give your best effort, you should be able to accumulate the two points required to win each tie."

Meike hadn't planned to play the Confederation Cup and still had no interest in competing. She didn't even know the complete list of teams in the field. But she didn't need to see which countries were sending teams to Paris and which weren't to know the Americans were the favorites.

Even if Helen's troublesome shoulder prevented her from taking the court, the pool of talented players the American coaches could choose from ran deep. Any team that included a combination of Alice Marble, Helen Hull Jacobs, Margaret

Osborne, or Dorothy Cheney would be difficult to beat. Meike felt confident she could win her singles matches, but given Liesel's inconsistent singles results, she didn't know if she could count on receiving enough support from her to earn the two points it would take to advance each day.

"If you do not abide by the terms I have laid out for you, it is my duty to inform you that you will be stripped of your amateur status and banned from future competition. The *Führer* is counting on a German victory in the Confederation Cup so we can demonstrate Aryan superiority for all the world to see. If you fail to deliver, you will be brought back here and your stay will not be as brief as it has proven to be during this visit." He slid a piece of paper toward her. "Please sign here to acknowledge your acceptance of these terms. Do you have any questions?"

"Just one." The last document Oskar had placed in front of her would have meant signing her life away. The document he was presenting now offered what might be her last chance to save it. "May I borrow a pen?"

❖

May 1938
Paris, France

Helen woke with a sour stomach and an attitude to match. It was nearly noon on the first day of the French Championships. The prestigious tournament was underway, but she was a spectator instead of a competitor. Not that she planned on attending any of the matches. Thanks to her vantage point in her friend Martine's apartment overlooking Roland Garros Stadium, she could sit in the living room window and see the action taking place on center court without having to subject herself to the prying eyes of the public. She wasn't ready to answer their questions—or to face her own.

She hadn't missed a major in years, but the tournament was going on without her this year. And according to the doctor she had seen when she arrived in Paris, it might not be the last. The doc said she might have played her last match, but she refused to think that way. She would play again. Perhaps not as well as before, but she would do whatever it took to rebuild her career. If Alice could come back from the brink of death, she could overcome this minor setback. Coming back from what she put Meike through? That would be much harder to achieve.

As Meike put her first round opponent out of her misery, Helen poured herself a cup of coffee and tried to tame the hangover she'd had every day since Meike discovered she had been acting as a spy. And a bad one at that.

She looked in the refrigerator for something to eat, but Martine and her lover Angelique, who spent the duration of the French Championships in Marseille each year to avoid the influx of tennis fans in Paris, hadn't left much behind. Just a carton of eggs, a package of cured ham, and something that might have been a bell pepper before time and Mother Nature turned it into something unrecognizable.

Helen scrambled some eggs and did her best to keep them down. She gave up after two bites. Opting for a little hair of the dog, she poured three fingers of bourbon into her coffee and waited for the pounding in her head to stop. A condition that was made exponentially worse by the sound of someone knocking on the door.

"How long do you intend to keep this up?" Swifty asked after she opened the apartment door to find him standing in the hall with a box of groceries in his arms.

"Until I have a reason not to."

"Then let me be the bearer of good news." He bulled his way inside and set the box of groceries on the kitchen counter. "I managed to convince the powers-that-be at the tennis association that you're healthy enough to play the Confederation Cup."

"Did they name me to the team?"

"Yes, but don't get too excited. They're not fully convinced your shoulder's up to snuff so they named you as an alternate."

"Which means I get to play dress-up and march into the stadium with the team in the opening ceremony, but I won't get to play unless someone gets hurt. The tournament's the first of its kind for amateur female tennis players, and the one I want to win more than any other. It would kill me not to be able to participate, Swifty."

He held up his hands in a gesture of helplessness. "I did what I could. The rest is up to you. You can start by drinking less of that and more of this." He took the cup of bourbon-spiked coffee from her and replaced it with a glass of fresh-squeezed orange juice.

"Slip some vodka or champagne into this, will you? That's the only way to make this stuff drinkable."

Swifty turned his back on her and began to put the groceries away. "Trust me. More booze is the last thing you need."

"Trust you?" Helen laughed dolefully. "Trust is in short supply these days." She watched him putter in the kitchen. "Does Lanier know how badly I screwed things up?"

"And how. The words 'international incident' came up a time or two during the course of our conversation. He's anxious to see you, but I told him I didn't know where you were."

She hadn't spoken to anyone since she'd left Rheinsteifel, but Swifty had known where to find her because she always used Martine and Angelique's apartment as her base of operations during the French Championships. Even though she wasn't playing the tournament this year, their generous offer still stood.

"If Lanier finds out you were lying to him," she said, "you can expect to be audited next year."

"Don't I know it." Swifty washed the crusty dishes in the sink and placed them in the strainer to drain. Then he dried his soapy hands on a dish towel and took a seat opposite her. "Talk to me, kid. Tell me you're going to pull out of this tailspin you're in."

Helen shook her head disconsolately. "I can't tell you what I don't know."

"What happened?"

"I already told you."

"Your telegram was skimpy on details, so tell me again."

"I could tell you the whole sob story, but it's easier if I give you the short version. I went to visit Meike in Germany, I spent some time with her and her family and I got to see who she really was. Unfortunately for me, she returned the favor."

"Sounds like you got sloppy and you got found out."

"I keep asking myself why I didn't toss the report before I gave my coat to Hans. I had six miles to get rid of it, but I forgot about the damn thing after the first few feet. I was so scared about making it through the tunnel without having it collapse on my head that I didn't give the report a second thought." She took a sip of her orange juice and winced as her queasy stomach rebelled against it. "I could tell Lanier it's his fault for insisting I put everything in writing, but I know the fault was mine. I got careless and I blew my cover. But I should have been honest with Meike from the beginning. Now she's through with me and I can't say I blame her. She was right about me all along. I don't take things seriously enough. If I did, I wouldn't be in the mess I'm in now. I wouldn't be sitting here wondering how I managed to screw things up with her a second time. All she wanted to do was love me and I just wanted to—What? Crack a few jokes? Make her laugh? Save my own hide?"

The challenge of melting Meike's icy exterior had been one of the things that had initially attracted Helen to Meike, but it was the warm, loving soul she had discovered under the surface that had drawn her in. Now Meike was gone for good. Helen stared at the orange pulp that had settled in the bottom of her glass.

"We could have had a future together, Swifty. Now all we'll ever have is a past."

"Dames." Swifty lit a Gauloise cigarette and blew out a thick plume of smoke that smelled almost as bad as the fumes produced by the cheap cigars he favored. "You can't live with them and you can't live without them."

"If I just had a chance to explain. Maybe I could make her understand why I did what I did. That's what I had planned to do when we got back to Rheinsteifel, but she read the report before I could prepare her for what was in it. Before I could tell her what I had been asked to do. You should have seen the look on her face when she discovered I had been spying on her and her family. She'll never trust me again, Swifty, let alone love me."

"You're forgetting something, kid. In tennis, love means nothing more than a goose egg on a scoreboard."

"And I've come out on the losing end once again."

"I'm going to give you some free advice. It's worth as much as you're paying for it, so you can take it or leave it." Swifty took one last puff of his cigarette and ground the unfiltered butt in an ashtray. "Don't chase after her. Give her some time to get over any hard feelings she might have toward you first."

"You're asking me to give her even more time to stew?"

"No, I'm asking you to give her time for the boil to cool to a simmer. She's pretty steamed at you right now and rightfully so. If I were in her shoes, I would rather slug you than forgive you. I've fixed a lot of situations for you in my time, kid, but I can't get you out of this one."

"I know. I sold out someone I love in order to save myself. A couple of sawbucks aren't going to cut it this time. What am I supposed to do?"

"I'm a businessman, not a relationship expert. Get yourself back in shape and get your career back on track. The Confederation Cup starts soon. That should come first and foremost. You can sort out the personal stuff later."

"Putting my career first is what started the ball rolling. I should have turned Lanier down when I had the chance and been woman enough to face the fallout when it came. Now it's too late. I'll never convince Meike to forgive me, no matter what I do or say." She nodded toward a week-old copy of a French newspaper. "According to that, she's decided to play the Confederation Cup. Why do you think she changed her mind?"

"I think a little guy with a funny-looking mustache probably twisted her arm. If not him, then someone under his command."

"You're probably right." Helen picked up the newspaper and stared at Meike's photo on the front page of the sports section. "I hope she knows what she's in for. She doesn't know what it's like to play for her country. The pressure's different. A player ranked one hundred can get so inspired, she can outclass a player ranked much higher."

"Do you think you can play?"

Helen tossed the newspaper aside. "I'm not only going to play. I'm going to win. Because I certainly don't have anything else to lose."

Chapter Ten

June 1938
Paris, France

Meike stood in the middle of the main show court at Roland Garros Stadium and held up the trophies she had earned for winning the singles and doubles titles at the French Championships. Liesel was ecstatic beside her and Inge was beaming from her seat in the stands, but Meike couldn't manage a smile. Although both of today's victories had been resounding, they felt hollow. She didn't feel the usual joy or sense of accomplishment she usually experienced during such moments. Only a grim satisfaction for having fulfilled her assigned duty to the Reich.

"Isn't this exciting?" Liesel asked as they continued to pose for the gathered photographers.

"Yes, it is."

"Then why don't you look happy?"

"This tournament might be over, but our work isn't done. The Confederation Cup begins in a few days."

The opening ceremonies were scheduled to take place Wednesday afternoon on the same court on which they were standing. The matches would begin the following day, culminating in next Sunday afternoon's final. Meike was grateful for the tight schedule. The condensed time frame would give her fewer chances to run into Helen off the court, but—provided Helen had returned to full-strength—meeting her on it seemed almost inevitable.

"If we play as well as we did today, the other teams won't stand a chance," Liesel said. "I'm hoping we play the Americans in the final, don't you? I want to exact some revenge on Helen Wheeler for teaming up to beat us in the doubles final in Australia."

Mindful of the reporters standing within earshot, Meike kept her voice low. "Has she recovered from her recent injury? I heard she might not even play next week."

"I don't think her injury was as serious as she made it seem," Liesel said with a sniff of disdain. "She probably pulled out of the French Championships so she could be fresh for the Confederation Cup. Then she probably asked the coaches to list her as an alternate so the other teams wouldn't know who they would have to face. Even though clay isn't her best surface, who in their right mind would leave the second-ranked player in the world sitting on the bench?"

"Do you think she's capable of such gamesmanship?" Meike wouldn't have thought so a few weeks ago, but one fateful night in Rorschach had turned everything she had thought she knew about Helen on its head.

"I wouldn't put it past her. She has always struck me as someone who wants to win at all costs. Not like you."

"No," Meike said, "she is nothing like me."

Despite their disparate backgrounds, she used to think she and Helen had so much in common. Now she realized they couldn't be more different. Or further apart.

"Meike," a reporter called out, "how do you plan to celebrate your latest victory?"

Meike switched from German to English. "I am happy to have won, but I do not have the luxury of being able to reflect on what I have done. The most important competition of my life begins on Thursday, and I want to make sure I am prepared to play my best tennis."

"In other words," Liesel said, "she will be limiting herself to one glass of champagne instead of two. But don't worry, boys, I will make sure none of it goes to waste."

While the other reporters jotted down Liesel's humorous response, the original questioner turned to Meike for a follow-up to his initial query. "Until recently, Meike, you weren't entered in the Confederation Cup. What made you decide to change your mind?"

Meike's gaze drifted to Oskar, who was seated next to Inge in the front row of the players' box. Her mood darkened as she remembered the strong-arm tactics he had used to bully her into submission. Subjecting her to the horrors of a concentration camp, putting a gun to her head, and threatening to take away her freedom if she didn't agree to his terms.

"Was it Hitler?" another reporter asked before Meike had time to formulate a response. "He has said he plans to attend on Sunday not *if* but *when* Germany wins the final. How do you feel about him guaranteeing a victory? Does that put more pressure on you to succeed or less?"

Meike chose to be diplomatic rather than give the reporter the headline he so obviously sought. "No one can put more pressure on me than I already exert on myself. I hope the *Führer*, like the other spectators in attendance, will enjoy the matches. And I hope, above all, that the best team will win. Now, if you will excuse us, gentlemen, Liesel and I have a tournament to prepare for."

"You are the only member of the team who has not become a member of the National Socialist Party," Liesel said as they headed for the locker room. "Party members are required to salute the *Führer* when they appear before him, and all German citizens are required to return the salute when it is presented to them. Will you give the salute if we compete in the final on Sunday? It could be considered a sign of disrespect if you refuse to comply."

The gesture was purely symbolic but fraught with meaning. Performing the Nazi salute was not only encouraged but expected. Doing so could ease the tremendous pressure on Meike's shoulders, but it would cost her one of the few things she had left: her good name.

❖

Even though she had already been named to the American Confederation Cup team, Helen felt like she was auditioning for a roster spot as she worked out under the watchful eye of team captain Jeanne Chisholm. Jeanne was a former national champion and the coach of rising star Betty Chambers, who had nearly beaten Helen out for the spot she was clinging to by her fingernails.

"What do you think?" Helen asked after she narrowly lost an 8-6 practice set to teammate Helen Hull Jacobs, a fellow Californian and one of her best friends on the tour.

Her arms folded across her chest, Jeanne tapped a finger against her pursed lips. "Understandably, it took you a few games to shake off the rust," she said thoughtfully, "but your serve doesn't have the same forcefulness I'm used to seeing. You managed to keep the score close by using instinct and guile rather than power. Our team has been named the top seed in the tournament. Depending on how the draw turns out in a few hours, we'll probably be playing Poland or Italy in the first round. Poland has Jadwiga Jedrzejowska, and Italy has Alessandra Mastroianni. JaJa made it to the semifinals of Wimbledon and the US Championships last year, and Alessandra just reached the final of the French Championships, a testament to how well she plays on clay. To be honest, I don't think you could beat either of them right now."

Helen started to point out that she was still number two in the world, but her grip on the ranking was growing more tenuous by the day. Her absence from the tour had cost her valuable rankings points. Now the rest of the field was closing fast. Since the Confederation Cup wasn't an officially sanctioned tournament, her performance in the event wouldn't help or harm her ranking. But it could go a long way to helping her regain the respect—and the fear—of her fellow players.

"I'm going to start you out in doubles," Jeanne said. "Is that okay with you?"

"I can't deny that being relegated to doubles feels like a slap in the face, but I'm willing to do whatever it takes to help the team in any way I can."

"I know. That's why I chose you in the first place. Now hit the showers and get changed. We have a draw ceremony to attend."

"Thanks, skipper."

Jeanne's instructional comments made Helen feel like she was a young player just getting started, but the pain in her right shoulder as she stood under the shower spray made her feel older than her years. She rubbed the aching joint as the water continued to run. The team was counting on her to contribute, and she didn't want to let them down. Citing fatigue after a valiant run to the semifinals of the French Championships, Alice had removed herself from contention for the Confederation Cup squad, leaving Helen, "the other Helen," and Dorothy Cheney to carry the flag.

Helen didn't expect the team to have any trouble in the first round. Despite her recent success in Paris, Alessandra had a history of coming up short in big matches, and her supporting cast wasn't strong enough to help her pull off the upset. But the road would get tougher from there. Depending on the draw, the US could face Great Britain in the second round and Germany or Australia in the final. Helen still couldn't understand why

Germany had managed only a paltry third seed. Yes, the Australians were loaded in the second spot, but they weren't that strong on clay, and Germany boasted the best player in the world playing on her best surface. That had to account for something.

Helen was rounding into shape. Her legs felt strong and her endurance was almost where she wanted it to be. If the team made the championship round, she expected to be on the court instead of the sidelines. But she had work to do if she wanted to make her appearance in the final round more than ceremonial. She needed to get a few matches under her belt before she would be ready to face Meike in singles or doubles, especially on clay.

"Hurry up, Wheeler." Jeanne's voice echoed off the tiled walls. "They're getting started."

Helen turned off the shower, dried off, got dressed, and slipped into the back of the press room as the organizers of the Confederation Cup concluded their speeches. She looked around the room while the speaker droned on to extend his time in the spotlight. All the coaches had gathered to watch the draw ceremony, but only a few players had deigned to attend. She nodded at Isabella Sanchez from Spain, Amelia Sanderson from Great Britain, and Margaret Wilson from Australia. When she locked eyes with one of the members of the German contingent, she forgot how to breathe.

Meike stared right at her. Right through her. Her eyes, like her ashen face, looked haunted. Oskar Henkel sat two seats away, which probably accounted for some of Meike's discomfort. Helen felt responsible for the rest.

"I'm sorry," she mouthed, but Meike turned away before she could get the words out.

"Are you okay, kid?" Swifty asked, his usually gruff voice filled with concern. "You look like you've seen a ghost."

Helen wrapped her arms around her middle to protect against a sudden chill. "I think I did."

❖

Meike could feel Oskar's eyes on her as he tried to gauge her reaction to seeing Helen for the first time since her brief incarceration in Dachau, but she forced herself to keep her swirling emotions at bay. The time off seemed to have done Helen a world of good. She looked fit. She looked rested. She looked...beautiful. Not that such things mattered anymore. Not that they ever would again.

Helen's attempt at an apology—if that's what she had been about to do before Meike turned her back on her—had come much too late. There was nothing Helen could do or say now. The damage she had inflicted was irreparable; her actions unforgivable.

"Is something wrong?" Oskar asked under his breath.

"No," Meike said tersely. "Everything is fine."

She tried to will the official conducting the draw to move faster as he placed two numbers in a hat. A beret, naturally, considering their location on the outskirts of Paris. The United States, Australia, Germany, Great Britain, France, Spain, Poland, and Italy were seeded one through eight. If the official pulled an even number out of the beret and the seeds held according to form, the Americans would play Great Britain in the semifinals. If the official pulled an odd number, the Americans would play a semifinal against Germany instead.

The press had made it no secret how they wanted the draw to go. They were clamoring for a US-Germany final so they could see the two highest ranked players compete for the title— and they weren't above suggesting the tournament organizers should rig the draw so their desired narrative could play out.

Meike had been instructed to win or else. If she wanted to hoist the championship trophy in a few days' time, she couldn't afford to care who she had to defeat along the way. She supposed she could exact a small measure of revenge if the Americans were her victims in the final—Helen had been talking about the Confederation Cup for months and her desire to win the event was almost palpable—but Meike doubted continuing her superiority over Helen on the court would make her feel any better about their fractured relationship off it. In fact, it might make her feel even worse.

Helen hadn't given her reasons for agreeing to act as a spy, but Meike suspected her decision had something to do with protecting her tennis career. No other explanation made sense. How ironic to think Helen had often accused her of putting tennis in front of everything and everyone else in her life when it was plain to see the opposite was true.

Michel LeGrand, the head of the Confederation Cup organizing committee, smiled as he placed his hand in the beret and shuffled the numbered chips inside.

"In the inaugural Confederation Cup," he said as he slowly withdrew his hand, "the United States will have…" After a dramatic pause, he revealed the chip in his hand. "Evens."

A satisfied murmur began in the area reserved for members of the press.

"The United States, Great Britain, Spain, and Italy will be on the top half of the draw," Michel said as one of his assistants placed the countries' names on the draw board behind him. "Australia, Germany, France, and Poland will be in the bottom half."

Meike looked at the draw board. The US would play Italy in the first round, Australia would play Poland, Great Britain would play Spain, and Germany had the misfortune of having to square off against France, the home team.

The crowd's reaction to Meike had been mixed when she won the French Championships the week before. Some had cheered vociferously for her, while others had greeted her with jeers and whistles. When she took the court against the French team on Friday, she had no doubt the reception she received would be less than cordial. Not for political reasons, but patriotic ones.

"My fellow committee members and I look forward to a fun and exciting event," Michel said. "Good luck to all the teams. We will see you tomorrow for the opening ceremonies."

Reporters surrounded Meike after Michel finished speaking. They peppered her with so many questions she didn't have time to answer one before she was hit with another.

"Are you excited about the event?"

"What did you think about the draw?"

"Do you think Germany deserved better than the third seed?"

"Do you think you can lead your team to the title?"

"If you do win, would you consider it your greatest victory?"

Meike held up her hands to bring the cacophony to an end. "As Monsieur LeGrand said, I look forward to a fun and exciting event."

"Helen," another reporter called out, drawing everyone's attention to the other side of the room, "how does your shoulder feel? Do you think it can withstand the rigors of playing on slow red clay?"

"How does it feel to be ranked number two in the world and be relegated to a supporting role on a team you were supposed to lead?"

Even though Helen tried not to show it, Meike could tell the last question rankled her. She knew because she knew Helen. Better, it turned out, than Helen knew her. She started to leave while the reporters' attention was focused elsewhere, but she wanted to hear Helen's response. She needed to know her frame of mind. Was Helen as upset about what had transpired between them as she was, or had she been able to laugh it off like she did everything else?

"I just want to do whatever I can to help the team," Helen said. "Every point counts, right?"

"How about a picture?" a photographer suggested. "Can we get a shot of you and Meike?"

"I don't think—" Meike began, wishing she had slipped out of the room when she had the chance.

"Sure," Helen said before Meike could finish. "Make sure you get my best side, though. I don't want to look bad standing next to someone as easy on the eyes as the champ here." She extended her hand when the laughter died down. "Hello, Meike."

"Hello, Helen. You are looking well."

Meike was disappointed to see Helen act so flippantly after everything that had happened the last time they were together. But based on Helen's past behavior, she knew she shouldn't be surprised. Helen still cared about the present instead of the future. And the past, in her mind, was something best forgotten instead of remembered. Not for Meike. For her, the past, the present, and the future were equally important. And she had once hoped Helen could be a part of all three. Now that hope was gone.

She reluctantly reached for Helen's hand. She feared she would no longer feel the connection she and Helen had once shared. And she feared even more that she would. When their palms slid across each other, their fingers gripped each other's hands, and flashbulbs popped all around them, she had never been so happy to feel nothing at all.

"I never thought I'd see you here," Helen said. "When last we talked—"

Meike held her smile in place as the insatiable photographers continued to take their pictures, but there was no mirth in her voice when she said, "Many things have changed since the last time we talked. My feelings for you, most of all." Unable to hold on to the pretense any longer, she abruptly released Helen's hand. "Good luck this week. I hope to see you on Sunday."

And if she got to the championship match, she had no doubt her team would win. They had to. Because she wasn't just playing for her country. She was playing for her life.

CHAPTER ELEVEN

June 1938
Paris, France

The flags circling the stadium fluttered in the breeze as Helen waited to walk onto center court with the rest of the members of her team. Just like at the Olympic Games, the teams would march into the stadium in alphabetical order with the home team granted the honor of entering last. Germany came first in French so Meike and her team would enter the stadium first, Helen and her cohorts would walk in somewhere in the middle of the proceedings, and the French would bring up the rear.

Meike was her team's flag bearer. The announcement had been greeted not with the respect afforded the other teams' flag bearers but speculation she had accepted the role to avoid having to give the Nazi salute when her country's national anthem was played. Helen hoped Meike saw the appointment as the honor it was instead of the convenient escape it afforded her.

She took a peek into the stands. She didn't expect to see many fans—it was the middle of the day during the workweek—but most of the seats were filled with smiling faces eagerly waiting for the players to appear.

"Everybody loves a parade."

She adjusted the fit of her red cap, which had been paired with a matching scarf, a blue blazer, and a white skirt to create a patriotic team uniform.

"*Bellissima*," Alessandra Mastroianni said as she got in a last-minute smoke. She had earned the nickname *La Duce* from her fellow players because, thanks to her full lips and jutting jaw, she bore an uncanny resemblance to Benito Mussolini.

"You, too, Alex. Good luck this week."

Alessandra ground her cigarette beneath the toe of her stylish black boot. "Since my team has been drawn to play yours tomorrow, I think my week will be rather short, don't you?"

Helen laughed, something that didn't come as easily as it once did. "No hard feelings though, right?"

"Not if you have dinner with me tonight. We haven't seen each other in months. We have a lot of catching up to do. What do you say we start over a bottle of Bordeaux?"

If it were any other tournament, Helen might have leaped at the chance to have a few hours of mindless escape. But the Confederation Cup was too important to begin with a hangover— or a guilty conscience. Her heart belonged to Meike, even if Meike didn't want to claim the prize.

"I can't. Jeanne has us on a curfew."

"My coach implemented one of those, too, but my teammates and I are treating it as more of a suggestion than a rule. Jeanne seems much less willing to look the other way, so I wouldn't cross her if I were you."

"I don't intend to."

"I will allow you to refuse my invitation this time, but when I come to New York for the US Championships in a few months, you owe me a rain check."

"You've got a deal."

When Helen returned to her team, she noticed an unexpected face had joined the ranks. Her heart filled her throat when Paul Lanier said, "Miss Mastroianni was right. You do look beautiful."

"What brings you to Paris, Agent Lanier?"

"I haven't heard from you lately. I missed your smiling face."

The few players Helen hadn't taken into her confidence about her personal life looked at her as if they were witnessing a lovers' tiff.

"What are you really doing here?" she asked after she drew Lanier a discreet distance away.

"I wanted to inform you in person you've been released from our agreement. Your days as a spy are over."

"Why? Because I screwed up the assignment?"

"No, because Meike von Bismarck isn't a Nazi."

Helen felt an overwhelming sense of relief, followed by a surge of anger. "How long did it take you to figure out what I've been telling you all along?"

"Since the Nazis arrested her and threw her into Dachau without bothering to wait for a trial."

The thought that Meike had been forced to experience the hardships of a concentration camp made Helen feel sick. And it made her betrayal feel that much worse. Meike thought Helen suspected her of being in league with the people who had put her through hell. "How did you find out she'd been arrested?"

"Her parents made inquiries to several officials regarding her whereabouts, which caught the attention of one of our sources."

"What did the source say?"

"That Meike was dragged from her home, treated like a prisoner for twenty-four hours, and then released."

"They wouldn't just let her go."

"They would if they got what they wanted from her."

"Which is?"

"Total obedience. She may not be one of them, but she's at their mercy."

Helen remembered the haunted look she had seen on Meike's face before yesterday's draw ceremony. Now she knew the reason for that look. It wasn't a broken heart that was to blame but a shattered spirit. "They broke her when she was in Dachau, didn't they?" Helen felt her own spirits flag when Lanier nodded in affirmation. "Isn't there something we can do to save her?"

"Yeah." Lanier got her hopes up, then dashed them just as quickly. "You can lose. Because if she doesn't win this tournament, she's as good as dead."

Helen pushed her way through the crowd of players, coaches, and hangers-on and stood in front of Meike until Meike met her eye. "When were you going to tell me?"

"Tell you what?"

"What you were up against," she said in a fierce whisper. "What they put you through."

Meike's eyes widened as she gasped in surprise. Her expression looked pained and, for a moment, Helen thought she might admit everything. Then Meike drew herself up tall, put on a brave face, and said, "My life isn't your concern, Helen."

"But your death certainly is, and I won't be responsible for it."

"What is she talking about, Meike?" Liesel asked in obvious confusion.

"Nothing," Meike said. "Every tournament is life and death to me. This one is no different. Play your game, Helen, and I'll play mine. The rest will take care of itself."

"Perhaps." Helen cupped her hand against Meike's cheek, not caring who might be watching. "But who will take care of you?"

❖

Meike didn't play her best tennis in the first round—Liesel's loss in the opening singles match, combined with the raucous partisan crowd had her nerves on edge as she struggled mightily against the French number one—but she played well enough in singles and doubles for the team to eke out a 2-1 victory and take the tie. Great Britain defeated Spain by the same score and the US cruised by Italy 3-0.

In the day's only upset, JaJa Jedrzejowska led her seemingly overmatched Polish squad past favored Australia 2-1. The Australians looked uncomfortable off the grass courts on which they excelled, but JaJa's play was so inspired, Meike thought she could have beaten them on any surface. Now it was up to her to make sure JaJa didn't repeat her heroics against Germany. Because in the semifinals, the United States would take on its Wightman Cup rival Great Britain and Germany would face Poland. JaJa was equally adept on grass as she was on clay. Meike knew she would have her work cut out for her on Saturday. Especially if JaJa played as well as she did today.

"Is it true what Helen said yesterday?" Liesel asked as they made their way to the locker room, where Inge and designated alternate Rilla Huber were awaiting their arrival. "Is your life in danger?"

Meike examined the strings on her favorite racquet. The catgut was fraying and she needed to get it restrung. But racquet stringing was an art no two practitioners performed the same way and she couldn't afford to get stuck with a hack. Not this week. Not when every set, every game, every point was so vital. "I had better do the job myself. Do you suppose the stringer's office is still open?"

"Stop pretending you didn't hear me and answer my question," the usually meek Liesel said with uncharacteristic force as she turned Meike to face her. "Has someone threatened you? Oskar wouldn't allow something like that to take place, would he?"

"It's Oskar who's leading the charge," Meike almost said before the doubt she heard in Liesel's voice managed—just barely—to convince her to hold her tongue. Liesel was in love, and Meike knew that, short of having Liesel bear witness to Oskar's heinous acts, there was nothing she could do or say to change Liesel's opinion of him. "How much do you know about him?"

Liesel's cheeks colored as she placed a protective hand over her slightly rounded belly. Meike hadn't noticed Liesel's weight gain before, but it seemed blatantly obvious now.

"You are carrying Oskar's child?"

"Yes." Liesel's lips curled into a proud smile. "We are to be married after the tournament ends. We planned to tell everyone about the baby when enough time had passed to make it prudent to do so."

"Do you plan to make the announcement before or after you retire from the tour?"

Liesel's blush deepened. "How did you know?"

"It seems logical that if you're starting a family, Oskar would want you to stay home to take care of it." *And raise even more Hitler Youth to goosestep in his footsteps.*

"Don't you want a family, Meike?"

"I already have one."

"You know what I mean. Not the family you were born into but one of your own making. Don't you see a husband and children in your future?"

If things didn't go her way the next few days, Meike didn't know how much of a future she would have.

"Tennis has been my life for so long, I haven't given much thought to what I might do when I stop. But even when I was a little girl, I never foresaw having a husband or children."

"But don't you want to grow old with someone?"

"More than anything." Meike blinked away the tears that sprang to her eyes at the thought of being robbed of the chance. Of the opportunities she had already missed out on with Helen. "I want to grow old with someone I love and who loves me in return." She thought of the moment in the tunnel when Helen had told her she loved her and she had foolishly believed it to be true.

"And you don't want that person to be a husband but someone like Helen." It sounded more like a statement than a question, but Liesel provided her own answer. "Not someone like Helen but Helen herself. I could see by the gentle way she touched your face yesterday how much she loves you. And you love her, too, don't you? You can tell me," she said when Meike didn't respond. "I'm your doubles partner."

This time, Meike didn't hold back. "You are also Oskar Henkel's fiancée."

"You're like a sister to me. I wouldn't—I *couldn't* denounce you. To anyone." Meike must have looked skeptical because Liesel fixed her with an earnest look and said, "I know you don't trust many people, including me. You have made that abundantly clear over the years. But I'm asking you to trust me now. I want to win the Cup as much as you do, but neither of us can do it without the other. We need each other, Meike, and the one thing that requires is trust. Do you trust me?"

"Yes," Meike said after giving the matter some thought. "I trust you with my life."

Chapter Twelve

June 1938
Paris, France

Dorothy Cheney was struggling. She had managed to defeat Italian Maria Lorenzi in her first round rubber in two tight sets, but she had just dropped the second set to Brit Anne Carter and the match was headed to a decider. No sure thing on any surface, but even more so on clay, where momentum could change at the drop of a dime.

"Come on, Dodo," Helen said from her perch on the sidelines. "You can do it."

Jeanne shouted a few encouraging words of her own, then took a seat next to Helen on the end of the team bench. "You were the best player on the court in yesterday's doubles match. And that's saying something, considering Jacobs has made the final of the French Championships twice and she used to own the US Championships until Meike came along."

Helen looked over at her old friend. Helen Hull Jacobs, who had been playing world-class amateur tennis for almost thirteen years, was twenty-nine now and hadn't won a Grand Slam singles title since Meike ascended to the top of the sport two years ago. Some said Jacobs's best tennis was behind her. Now they were saying it about Helen, too. The Confederation Cup offered both a chance—perhaps their last chance—to prove everyone wrong. But how could Helen hope to win if the possible cost to Meike could prove so dear?

"How does your shoulder feel?" Jeanne asked after Dodo fought off two break points to hold serve and draw even at one-all in the third set.

"Good as new." Jeanne's arched eyebrow prompted Helen to amend her response. "Well, practically. Why do you ask?"

Jeanne turned back to the action on court and ran her hands through her short salt-and-pepper hair. "Dodo's twenty-one and the future of American tennis, but I don't think she's ready to face this kind of pressure yet. I picked her for the Confederation Cup team because she's excelled in Wightman Cup play the past two years, but she hasn't been playing with the same kind of confidence this week. In fact, she looks scared to death." As if to illustrate Jeanne's point, Dodo flubbed an easy overhead to fall behind 2-1. "If we win today," Jeanne said as the players changed ends, "I want you and Jacobs to play singles and doubles tomorrow. I want you to be my number one and Jacobs to play number two."

"But Jacobs has a better record on clay than I do."

"I know, but my gut says putting you in the top spot is the right call. The one that gives our team the best chance to win. You're not just due against Meike. You're overdue. It's your time. I can feel it."

The thought of playing Meike with the stakes as high as they were struck fear in Helen's heart. She found herself torn between rooting for Dodo to clinch the team's berth in the final and hoping the youngster would lose. She wanted to win the Confederation Cup, but she couldn't do it at Meike's expense.

"You don't know what you're asking me to do, Jeanne."

"Yes, I do. I'm asking you to fulfill your destiny. I've never seen a player who is more athletically gifted than you are and I've seen them all. From Suzanne Lenglen to Helen Wills Moody to

Alice Marble. You were put on this earth to play tennis, Helen. You were born to win big matches and I can't think of any more important than the one you could play tomorrow afternoon."

A match Meike couldn't afford to lose and Helen couldn't afford to win.

❖

The roar from the center court crowd forced Meike, playing on an adjacent court, to let the ball drop instead of following through with her serve. She stepped away from the baseline and turned to Inge for confirmation of what she already suspected: the United States had just beaten Great Britain to advance to the championship round. Helen and her teammates were going to play for the Confederation Cup.

Meike tried and failed to suppress a smile. Despite the recent friction between them, she was proud of what Helen had managed to accomplish this week. In a few short days, she had completely rehabilitated her image in the eyes of the press and fans. She had proved she could be unselfish, putting the team's success ahead of her individual achievements. Even though Dorothy Cheney had struggled in singles, Helen hadn't lobbied to take her place. She had been nothing but supportive of her teammate despite the press's attempts to bait her into saying something negative. Her play, both in practice and in live competition, had been sparkling, even though the powerful serve she was known for seemed to have gone missing. Now she was one day away from being praised for her tennis instead of scorned for her temper.

And it was Meike's job to prevent it from happening. To stop Helen from having her day so she could have her own tomorrows.

She glanced at her family sitting in the stands. Her parents had barely left her side since she was returned to them after her trip to Dachau, and her brother had taken time off from his studies in order to come to Paris to offer his support. The three of them smiled to offer their encouragement, but she could see how nervous they were. They knew just as well as she did what losing this event could cost her. She smiled back, then returned to the task at hand.

She held up a hand to apologize to her opponent for the delay in play. JaJa Jedrzejowska nodded her acceptance and assumed her return stance. Meike had beaten JaJa at two Grand Slam events the year before and JaJa seemed determined to make up for those losses today. She had held serve easily in the opening game of the match and had Meike in a 0-30 hole in the second.

Meike took a deep breath to steady herself. Liesel's win against Agnieszka Rosolska in the previous match had taken some of the pressure off her, but she couldn't afford to let down her guard. If JaJa managed to pull off the upset in singles, Poland could still win the tie if they won the doubles match to follow. Meike needed to clinch the tie now on her first opportunity and not risk getting into a winner-takes-all match against a team with nothing to lose and everything to gain.

JaJa bounced on the balls of her feet, revealing her growing confidence. She had never beaten Meike, but each of their matches had been close. Meike didn't expect today to be any different. Not when the resulting victory wouldn't be routine but career-defining.

"Break down her strength instead of her weakness," Meike said under her breath, "and the match is yours."

Most of JaJa's opponents directed their shots to her backhand because they were afraid of getting beaten by her ferocious forehand. Meike knew JaJa would hit her share of winners off her forehand wing, but perhaps she would make a few costly errors, too.

She directed her serve to JaJa's forehand and the majority of the groundstrokes that followed. JaJa seemed surprised by the tactic and made four forehand errors to give Meike the game.

The errors kept coming in the next game, which Meike won to break serve and pull ahead 2-1. She relaxed once she got the lead. Her shots began to come more freely and JaJa began to miss more than she made.

Meike won the first set 6-2. JaJa put up a fight in the second set, battling back from a break down to briefly take the lead, but Meike settled down and won the set 7-5 to seal the victory and clinch the tie.

She would live to play another day.

CHAPTER THIRTEEN

June 1938
Paris, France

As the rest of the team chowed down in the dining room of their hotel, Helen stared at the steak she had ordered but couldn't eat. She had moved into the Hotel Parisienne before the Confederation Cup began because her teammates and coaches planned to set up shop there during their stay in Paris, but she found herself longing for the solitude of Martine and Angelique's apartment. She loved a party as much as the next girl, if not more, but tonight she wanted to be alone.

"What's the matter, kid," Swifty asked as he cracked into a lobster claw, "lost your appetite?"

"I've got to see her."

Swifty's jaw dropped so far it nearly ended up in the container of drawn butter resting next to his oversized dinner plate. "There are Nazis crawling all over the German team's hotel and the head man himself is on his way. What are you trying to do, get yourself killed the night before the biggest match of your life?"

"No, I'm trying to ease my mind." She lowered her voice so the rest of the team couldn't hear her. Not that she needed to concern herself about that. Her teammates were so keyed up about today's win and tomorrow's final, their excited conversations easily drowned out her whispered one. "I need to know if she's okay. I need to know what she's thinking."

"I'm sure she's thinking the same thing you are. If she wins, she lives. If she doesn't..." Swifty shrugged and let his voice trail off.

"That's why I need to see her tonight. Because tonight might be my last chance to get her alone. I have to tell her I'm throwing the match."

"You're what?" Swifty looked like the sure thing he'd bet a wad of dough on had come in last instead of first. "Don't be crazy, kid."

"I'm not, Swifty. What I am is in love."

"Same thing." He waved his fork in the air and nearly dropped an asparagus spear on the immaculate linen tablecloth. "Now eat your dinner and stop spouting nonsense."

"She's staying at the Metropole, isn't she?"

Swifty nearly choked on his glass of wine. "You're joking, right?" he asked, wiping chardonnay off his chin.

"I've never been more serious. Now are you going to help me or not?"

He rolled his eyes heavenward. "I always knew you were going to be the death of me one day, but I didn't figure today would be the day."

Helen grinned. "So is that a yes?"

Swifty tossed his napkin on the table and grabbed a bottle of wine for the road. "Come on, kid. Let's go."

❖

Meike stared out her hotel room window at the silhouette of the Eiffel Tower etched against the background of the darkening sky. The view was so beautiful it brought tears to her eyes. But these days, it didn't take much to bring her emotions to the surface. Simply seeing Michael and her parents playing a game of hearts like they were now was enough to reduce her to tears. Her tennis career had made moments like this the exception rather than the rule and she found herself mourning for what might have been. Longing for what still might be.

A brisk knock on the door made her stiffen in dread and brought the cheerful chatter at the card table to an end.

"Room service," a female voice called out in serviceable French that bore the slight trace of an American accent.

Meike and her family shared anxious looks, each silently asking the other if they had placed an order but fully aware the answer was no.

Another knock brought Meike's father out of his seat.

Meike stepped away from the window. "No, Papa. I will go."

"Room service," the voice said again.

"Just a moment, please. I'm coming." Meike crossed the room and cautiously opened the door. The SS guards who were normally stationed at each end of the hall flanked a woman in a hotel employee's uniform. The woman was standing behind a room service cart laden with a vase of flowers, an ice-filled bucket of champagne, and a dome-covered tray.

"Your dinner, Miss von Bismarck," the woman said.

Meike was so shocked to see Helen standing in the hall, she nearly said her name out loud. "Thank you. Please come in." She opened the door wider and ushered Helen inside. "You shouldn't be here," she said, switching from French to English after she closed the door behind them.

"I know, but I had to see you."

Meike's mother rushed toward Helen and slapped her across the face. Helen's cheek reddened as a result of the forceful blow. "Do you still think my daughter is a Nazi?" she asked as Meike's father prevented her from taking another swing.

"Mama, please." Meike motioned toward the door, reminding her mother the real enemy was on the other side.

"It's okay, Meike." Helen rubbed the palm-shaped mark on her cheek. "I deserved that smack and a whole lot worse. But I didn't come here tonight to be anyone's punching bag. I came hoping you would give me a chance to explain."

Meike's father led her mother to the open door between their adjoining rooms and motioned for Michael to follow. "We shall leave you alone so you can talk."

"How did you get past the guards?" Meike asked after her family had taken their leave. "Where did you find that uniform? What—"

"Wait. Hold on. One question at a time." Helen placed a finger against Meike's lips to stem the flood. Then she took Meike's hands in hers. Unsure if she was ready to hear what Helen planned to say, Meike allowed herself to be led to a nearby sofa. "We don't have long, so I'd better make it fast. Swifty and I bribed one of the maids into taking an hour off, but I need to clear out before the big galoots in the hallway get suspicious."

"What are you doing here, Helen? It isn't safe. What if Oskar were to see you?"

"I know how dangerous it is for me to be here, but I had to see you, Meike. I had to let you know why I did what I did."

"Why you spied on me, you mean?"

Meike tried to pull away, but Helen held her fast.

"I can't blame you for being angry with me. I would be, too, if I were you." Helen paused as if she needed to build her courage to say what was on her mind. What was in her heart. "A man came to see me back in December. He said he was from my government and he needed my help. He wanted me to get close to you so I could find out what you knew about Hitler's plans and how they would affect our country. He wanted me to keep tabs on you, too, to make sure you weren't one of them."

"Why would he think that?"

"He showed me pictures of you entering and leaving Nazi headquarters and he said he thought you were one of Hitler's allies."

"I'm not."

"I know that now. I knew it then, too, but the boys in Washington didn't want to take my word for it. They wanted proof. Proof they wanted me to get. I didn't want to do what they asked, but they had pictures. Compromising pictures of me and you. If I didn't do what they asked, they would have exposed both of us. I could have ended up in jail and you might have ended up in—"

"Dachau?" Meike finally managed to free herself from Helen's grasp. "I'm afraid your efforts to protect me came up woefully short, Helen, but at least you were able to save yourself."

Helen's eyes pleaded for mercy. "Can you ever forgive me?"

Meike examined her heart. If she had to die, she didn't want to go to her grave holding a grudge. Especially against the woman she loved. "There is nothing left to forgive." She stroked Helen's unruly curls as she finally let go of the animosity she had felt toward her since that fateful night in Rorschach. As she allowed her true feelings to rise to the surface. "I would be in the predicament I am in now with or without the deal you made all those months ago." Helen looked as if she had just been spared from the gallows. Meike, meanwhile, felt the noose around her own neck grow even tighter. "Just tell me one thing. Did you mean what you said that night in the tunnel? Did you mean it when you said you loved me?"

Helen nodded fervently. "Of course I did. I love you more than life itself, Meike."

"Then promise me something."

"Anything."

"Promise me you won't treat our match tomorrow any different from the rest we've played. Promise me you will play to win and not to lose."

"Meike, I can't do that. Not if winning could cost you your life."

"Promise me, Helen."

Helen's eyes were a swirl of colors—and emotions. But the sentiment that came through clearest was love. "I promise."

"Thank you." Meike held Helen's face in her hands and kissed her like she might never get the chance again. She memorized the feel of her lips, the taste of her skin, and the warmth of her touch. Then she pulled away. "Please leave before I won't be able to let you go." She turned her back and returned to the window, unable to watch Helen walk out of her life for what might be the last time.

"Good night, Meike."

Meike's tears began to fall even before she heard the door click shut. "Good-bye, my love."

Chapter Fourteen

12 June 1938
Paris, France

The day dawned gloomy and overcast. The conditions were even heavier by the time the teams lined up on center court, the sky filled with dark gray clouds portending rain. A hot, dry day would have made the balls fly faster through the air. On a day like today, the crushed brick court would be molasses slow, making it hard to generate pace and nearly impossible to attack the net. Perfect for a baseliner but terrible for a serve-and-volleyer. Advantage, Germany.

"The weather gods may be against us, but it sounds like we have the crowd on our side," Helen said as she took a long look at the foreboding sky.

"Not all of it."

Helen followed Jacobs's line of sight. She couldn't believe her eyes when she took a gander at one of the spectators standing in the front row of the VIP box. Adolf Hitler himself was chatting animatedly with several of his underlings.

"My God, the bastard actually came."

He looked smaller than he did on the newsreels, where he seemed to tower over everyone else in the frame, but the force of his personality allowed him to hold sway over the yes-men surrounding him now. Heinrich Himmler, Oskar Henkel, and the rest of the toadies who blindly followed his orders hung on every word as he punched the air with his fists as if he were giving a speech to tens of thousands instead of speaking casually with a relative few while waiting for a tennis match to begin.

"He predicted a German victory and he's here to see it come true. Well, let's give him a show he won't forget." Jacobs peeled off her sweater and draped it across one of the lower rungs of the umpire's chair. She took a sip of hot tea for fortification and offered Helen a drink, but Helen waved her off in favor of something stronger. She hated the idea of Hitler celebrating a German victory, but she needed to make sure he got what he wanted so Meike could live.

As she drank from a flask of brandy, Helen sneaked a peek at Meike out of the corner of her eye. If Meike was nervous or anxious about the upcoming matches, she didn't show it. Her face was calm, her expression stoic. She looked ready to face her fate—whatever that might turn out to be.

Helen needed to keep the tie close so no one—not even Meike—could know the fix was in. She didn't want to let her team down, but she didn't see any other way.

She tapped the head of one racquet against the strings of another to test the tension. The order of play had been reversed for today's final, and the doubles match was up first instead of last so it could serve as an appetizer rather than a potential afterthought. The number two singles players would square off when the doubles match ended, and the number one players would close the show. The organizers were probably hoping for a split in the first two matches so Helen and Meike's match would have more meaning. Helen was hoping for the opposite. If the tie was already decided by the time she and Meike faced each other, they wouldn't have anything to play for. Helen wouldn't have to worry about winning or losing. Only trying to save face—or finding a way to save Meike's life.

The Germans won the racquet flip and elected to return, a risky proposition considering Helen and Jacobs had two of the best serves in women's tennis. But Meike and Liesel returned beautifully and broke serve without conceding a point. Then Meike held at love to stake her team to a quick 2-0 lead. The match had just begun and it already seemed to be over.

"Slow down," Jeanne called from the sidelines. "You can't win the match in the first couple of games."

Jacobs's sterling play at the net helped Helen hold serve and pull the team within a game, but Meike's play was even better and Liesel was returning out of her mind.

"Who does she think she is, Don Budge?" Jacobs asked after Liesel whistled a winner past her to help Germany break serve for the second time. "I've never seen a woman hit a forehand that hard."

"The way she's playing today, I think she could teach Budgie a thing or two."

"Surely she can't keep it up."

To Jacobs's chagrin, Liesel continued to play spectacularly well. Both in doubles and in singles. Liesel and Meike won the doubles match 6-3, 6-2 and, after a short rest period to allow the players to catch their breaths, Liesel raced out to a 5-0 in the first set of the number two singles match. Jacobs managed to hold serve to keep from getting whitewashed, but Liesel closed out the set 6-1. The Germans were one set away from winning the Confederation Cup. In the stands, Hitler was practically doing a victory dance. So was Helen. If Liesel played the second set as well as she did the first, the tie would be over in a matter of minutes. And Meike would be safe.

But Jacobs fought back. Instead of getting down on herself for losing the first set so handily, she got angry. "I'm going to wipe the smile off his face if it's the last thing I do," Helen heard her grumble as the players changed ends at the start of the second set.

When play resumed, Jacobs didn't resemble the player who hadn't won a Grand Slam singles title in two years. She looked like the one who had once won the US Championships four years running. And Liesel slowly began to revert to form, waiting for her opponent to make an error instead of forcing the action. The tactic might have worked in the first set when Jacobs couldn't find the court. But in the second set, Jacobs couldn't miss.

"Liesel's done. This match is ours." Jeanne knelt in front of Helen after Jacobs took the second set 6-2 and surged to a 4-0 lead in the third. "The tie is in your hands now. Are you ready to play the most important match of your life?"

"Yes, I am," Helen said, and when it was over, she hoped her teammates would be able to live with the result.

❖

Meike's hands were shaking. She was always nervous before an important match, but not like this. Never like this.

She closed her eyes and tried to let everything fall away. The crowd murmuring in anticipation of the final match, Liesel berating herself for letting her nerves get the best of her against Helen Hull Jacobs, Inge delivering last-minute instructions. But she couldn't block out the sounds. She heard everyone and everything. Including the doubts running through her mind. She had been perfect for so long—unbeatable for match after match—but could she do it again? Could she come through when it really counted?

Helen could have beaten her in Australia, but Helen's serve had abandoned her at the start of the second set and her composure had followed. Helen wasn't serving as powerfully as she had in Australia, but her placement was better and her ground game seemed much more thoughtful. She was a different player than she had been in January. And a better one. But knowing what was at stake, would she be able to relax and play the kind of tennis that had put her team on the brink of winning the Confederation Cup? She hadn't played well in today's doubles match and she hadn't played a singles match on clay in over a year. The odds were on Meike's side. But why did she feel like she was holding a losing hand?

"Play your game," she told herself as the sounds finally began to fade, "and everything will be fine."

❖

Swifty cupped his hands around his mouth to amplify his voice. "If you win this match, kid, I'll make you a mint."

"What about me, Mr. Anderson?" Meike asked with a Mona Lisa smile. "What will you do for me if I win?"

Helen welcomed the much-needed moment of levity. "He can't make you famous, champ. You already are."

Swifty's belly bobbed as he laughed from deep within. The English-speaking spectators within earshot also laughed at the exchange, but Gladys Morton, the chair umpire who had been a thorn in Helen's side for most of her career, was not amused.

"I will not stand for any of your usual shenanigans today, Miss Wheeler." Gladys wagged a prudish finger. "If you do not behave with the utmost decorum, I will punish you accordingly."

"So I shouldn't count on any close calls going my way. Is that what you're saying?"

The lines between Gladys's beady little eyes deepened into a furrow. "My reputation for integrity is unassailable, Miss Wheeler, which is more than I can say for yours."

Helen bit back a rejoinder that might have gotten her disqualified from the match before the first point was played. Pick your battles, she told herself. Today, the most important one was between the lines, not outside them.

"May I?" Gladys borrowed one of Meike's racquets and held the head of it against the ground. "Up or down?" she asked, indicating the manufacturer's logo on the butt of the racquet. Meike chose up, but when Gladys spun the racquet and let it fall, it landed with the logo pointing down. "You have won the toss, Miss Wheeler. Would you prefer to serve or return?"

The decision would have been easy to make under normal circumstances. She would choose to serve and try to stake herself to an early lead while her opponent was still trying to shake off early-match jitters. But these were definitely not normal circumstances.

"I'll return."

Gladys turned to Meike. "From which side of the court would you prefer to serve?"

Meike glanced at the sky. No one liked to serve with the sun's glare in her eyes. But with so much cloud cover, the sun wouldn't be a factor. "I'll take that one."

By opting to serve from the north end, Meike would begin the match with her back to Adolf Hitler. Gladys might not have noticed the snub, but Helen certainly did.

So much for total obedience.

"This match isn't about the people watching it," Meike said. "It's about the people playing it."

And only they could decide the outcome.

❖

"Quiet, please," Gladys Morton said after she took her seat in the umpire's chair. "The players are ready."

The buzzing crowd obediently grew silent. Meike had never seen an audience of thousands make so little noise. But by the looks on their expectant faces, they wouldn't remain silent for long. They were waiting for a chance to come alive. To cheer for their chosen favorite. Since Helen was the underdog, Meike expected the crowd to be on her side. But when she won the first point after an extended baseline rally, the crowd roared its approval.

The second point was just as drawn out, but it went in Helen's favor after she drew Meike out of position and hit a crackling forehand winner.

Before she served the next point, Meike looked across the net and caught Helen's eye. Not to search for signs of weakness but to share the moment. She smiled when she saw her own feelings reflected on Helen's face. If each point was like the first two, they were about to play a match for the ages.

Helen had run out to a quick lead in Australia as she practically served Meike off the court, but it was a different story in Paris. The first set was nip and tuck all the way. Each game was tightly contested, with neither player seeming to hold an advantage.

"I beat her at her own game in Adelaide," Meike said to herself after Helen won yet another baseline rally to pull even at five-all. "Now she's trying to beat me at mine."

When Helen reached triple break point in the next game, she seemed close to succeeding. But Meike bore down and hit a string of winners to pull herself out of danger. Temporarily. Helen ran through her next service game to pull even again, then attacked the net at every opportunity. Was Helen trying to shorten the points to disrupt Meike's rhythm or was she starting to tire? Meike didn't have time to give the matter too much thought because Helen broke her to take the lead. Then, fueled by adrenaline and momentum, she hit three aces and a service winner to win the set 8-6.

A little over an hour ago, Liesel had put Germany one set away from the Confederation Cup. A short time later, the teams' fortunes had been reversed and it was Helen and the Americans who were close to claiming the crown.

Meike had come from a set down to win the Australian Championships. Now she would have to do it again. Except this time there was more than a title on the line.

❖

Helen could see her teammates jumping out of their seats, but she didn't join the celebration. Her loss in the final of the Australian Championships had taught her not to lose confidence even if things weren't going her way. And winning the first set of the deciding match in the Confederation Cup final had taught her something else: she could beat Meike von Bismarck and maybe, just maybe, she could save her, too.

"Do I need to remind you that play is supposed to be continuous?" Gladys asked after Helen jogged over to the sidelines.

Helen heeded the warning note in Gladys's voice and resolved to keep her conversation with Swifty as brief as possible so she wouldn't end up getting penalized for it. "Where's Lanier?"

Swifty raised his hands to the sky. "Who do I look like, his keeper?"

"Find him for me, will you? I need to run something by him."

"Now? In the middle of the match?" Not wanting to say too much in front of the spectators listening in, Helen pleaded with him with her eyes. "Okay, okay." Swifty began to edge his way past the fans between him and the aisle. "The things I do for you."

Helen blew him a kiss. "I love you, Swifty."

"Are you ready to resume play, Miss Wheeler," Gladys asked, "or do you need time to declare your love to someone else?"

"I'm ready," Helen said. And if her plan worked out, she and Meike would have all the time in the world.

❖

Helen was doing almost as much running around between games as she was during them. Each time they changed ends, she ventured to the sidelines to talk to Swifty and a man in a dark gray suit. The man looked vaguely familiar, but Meike didn't recognize him right away. After she held serve to take a 4-3 lead in the second set, she finally realized where she had seen him before. He was the man who had asked Helen for her autograph in the lobby of the Waldorf Astoria the night Helen had taken her to the Cotton Club. He had pretended to be a star-struck fan that night, but he was obviously much more.

"He must be her handler." Blessed with the clarity of hindsight, Meike could finally see him for who he really was.

Helen had said her days as a spy had come to an end. But if that were truly the case, what was her handler doing here and why was she seeking his counsel in the middle of play?

"Concentrate on the match," she told herself after Helen held serve for four-all. "Don't worry about questions you can't answer."

Like in the first set, she had the advantage of serving first. The longer she held the lead, the more chances she had to force Helen to stumble. All she needed to do was keep holding her serve, put some pressure on Helen's, and make sure she didn't falter late in the set like she had in the first. If she repeated her mistake, the match would be over. Helen would win and she would lose. In more ways than one. But if she could hold her nerve and wait for Helen to lose hers, the set—and the match—could be hers.

A few games later, Meike held serve to pull ahead 6-5. On the first point of the following game, Helen got her first serve in and came in behind it. The serve was placed well but didn't have much on it and Meike returned it easily. She clenched her fists when the ball flew past Helen's outstretched racquet and dropped in the corner for a winner. Love-fifteen.

"You can do it, Meike."

Her brother's shout of encouragement turned Meike's attention to her family in the stands. She didn't normally need anyone's support to help her win, but today she'd never needed her family's more. What was it Helen had said on their last night in Rheinsteifel? *Everyone needs someone sometime.* For her, that time was now. She had gone as far as she could on her own. She couldn't go any further without help.

Talent and skill could take her close to her goal but wouldn't allow her to reach it. If she wanted to win today, she would need heart. Pluck. Virtues normally attributed to her opponent. If she wanted to defeat Helen, she needed to become Helen. She smiled at the absurdity of the thought. The beauty of the compliment.

Helen served-and-volleyed on the second point, too. On clay, one serve-and-volley point during a game might be considered a surprise tactic; two could only be seen as a sign of desperation. The pace of Helen's shots had started to wane in the past few games and her forays to the net were becoming more frequent and ill-advised. She, like Meike, was playing her fourth set of the day. Had she finally begun to tire or had her shoulder injury flared up again?

Meike searched Helen's face for signs of weakness but saw only determination. In Australia, Helen's only strategy had been to hit every ball as hard as she could. The strategy had worked when her shots were going in, but when she had started to miss, she hadn't been able to adjust. In Paris, her game plan was more cerebral and gave her a much higher margin of error, which kept the match agonizingly close.

Instead of hitting the ball flat or coming over it to generate high-bouncing topspin, Helen used slice to keep the ball low. The crowd *ooh*-ed as her groundstrokes passed mere centimeters above the net. Meike's heart leaped into her throat each time the ball skimmed the orange-dusted tape on its way over. She kept waiting for Helen to miss, but she kept waiting in vain. After a thirty-stroke rally, she finally got what she was waiting for. Helen's slice backhand caught the tape, hung tantalizingly in the air for a moment as if held aloft by the crowd's collective gasp, then dropped on Helen's side of the net. Love-forty. Meike was a point away from leveling the match.

"Yes!"

Meike clenched her fists as the crowd roared. She couldn't tell if the fans were cheering for her to win or hoping to see another set of wonderful tennis, but she had the opportunity to give both factions what they wanted and she meant to take it. But Helen served an ace to save one set point and hit a service winner to stave off another. Meike, holding up a hand to ask for more time to prepare, vowed not to let the third go begging.

"This is your chance," she told herself as she crept closer to the baseline. "Take it."

At 30-40, Helen opted for placement instead of pace. Meike stepped to her left, cut off the angle, and hit a crosscourt backhand that would have been a winner on any day except this one—and against any other player except Helen. Helen ran down the shot with ease, hit a looping backhand to give herself time to recover, and scrambled to the middle of the court to await Meike's reply.

Meike waited for the high-arcing ball to land. Instead of going for an outright winner to try to end the point quickly, she settled in for yet another extended rally. She moved Helen from side to side, sapping her energy and exhausting her legs. If successful, the tactic could not only win her the second set but the third as well.

Helen's grunts of effort grew louder on each stroke, giving voice to her fatigue, but she stubbornly hung in the point. Meike admired her grit. Helen was playing like a dream on a surface that had given her nothing but nightmares. When Meike hit a forehand that Helen's weary legs couldn't catch up to, Meike's own dream came true. She arched her back and unleashed a roar that nearly rent the heavens. She had pushed the final match of the Confederation Cup to a deciding set.

"Game and second set, Germany," Gladys said. "Play will resume in thirty minutes."

The crowd rose as one to salute the players as Meike and Helen gathered their belongings and headed to the locker room for the rules-mandated break between the second and third sets. Meike didn't want to stop playing now that she had finally gained some momentum, but the decision was out of her hands.

The Davis Cup was the only event that allowed a stoppage of play during matches. Players traditionally took a respite between the fourth and fifth sets to give themselves time to strategize with their coaches before the deciding set began. The organizers of the Confederation Cup had decided to implement something similar.

Meike waved to the cheering fans, then headed to the locker room to prepare herself to play a set that could define not only her legacy, but her life.

❖

Helen's right arm felt like a bowl of overcooked spaghetti noodles. Her lack of match play had started to catch up with her. Her shoulder was shot and her legs weren't too far behind. Yet she had never felt so happy.

If she put her plan into action now instead of waiting until the Cup had been decided, no one would ever see it coming. Not Henkel. Not Himmler. Not Hitler. Not even her teammates.

"I have a proposition for you, ladies. And I'll say right off the bat you aren't going to like it."

"I would tell you to keep it to yourself," Jacobs said, "but I've known you long enough to know that's not going to happen, so spill."

Helen stood and addressed her team. "If Meike doesn't win this match, the consequences for her will be dire."

Indignant, Jeanne put her hands on her hips. "So what are you going to do, roll over and let her win? Please tell me you're not planning to throw the final set."

"No, skip, I'm not. In fact, I'm not going to play it at all. And if I can talk some sense into Meike, neither is she."

Dodo scratched her head. "You've lost me."

"The Nazis will be all over this place the minute the match ends, no matter who wins. At the moment, though, they're too busy planning their celebration to keep tabs on Meike. If I'm going to help her escape, I need to get her out of here and I need to get her out of here now. But I can't do it without your help. And I won't do it unless it's something each of you agrees to do."

"Do you know what kind of sacrifice you're asking us to make?" Jacobs asked.

"Yes, I do." Helen looked each of them in the eye one by one. "I'm asking you to give up your dreams of being a member of the first team to win the Confederation Cup. I'm asking you to forego front-page headlines, a hero's welcome, and a ticker tape parade down Madison Avenue. I'm asking you to help me save a friend."

"If we do what you're asking," Dodo said, "we'll still be heroes. We just won't be treated like it."

"The decision has to be unanimous," Helen said. "If there's even one dissenting vote, I will go back out there and finish the match. But I have to admit I won't be playing to win."

Jeanne raked her hands through her hair. "It's the goddamn Confederation Cup. Don't you want to win?"

"Of course I do, but there's more to life than tennis. And without Meike, I would have no life at all."

"If you play the deciding set," Jacobs said, "what would happen to Meike after the match ended?"

"Even if she wins, she loses. There'll be guards at every exit and she won't be able to take a step without someone walking in her shadow. If we're going to make a move, we need to do it now. But whatever you decide, that's what I'll do. No questions asked and no hard feelings held. What do you say?"

Jacobs, Dodo, and Jeanne looked at each other but didn't speak. Helen bit her lip as she waited for them to come to a decision. Finally, Jacobs slapped herself on the knee and said, "I don't need this trophy. I already have enough hardware. Count me in."

Dodo shrugged and said, "There's always next year."

Helen turned to Jeanne. "That leaves you, skip. What do you say?"

Jeanne was understandably slow to respond. With no Grand Slam champions in her coaching stable and none on the horizon, winning the Confederation Cup could be the pinnacle of her career. "Adding you to this team was the best decision I've ever made. And the decision you're asking me to make now is the hardest." Jeanne's voice shook as she squeezed Helen's shoulder and said, "What do you need me to do?"

"Distract Inge so she doesn't sound the alarm."

"What about Liesel? She and that guy Henkel seem pretty tight."

"You're right. I don't know if she can be trusted. Let's keep her in the dark for now. Getting Meike on our side is more important."

"And how do you intend to do that?"

Helen scribbled a note on a piece of paper and pressed it into Jeanne's palm. "Give her this. Just don't let anyone see you do it."

"You're pretty good at subterfuge," Jacobs said. "Have you been moonlighting as a spy or something?"

"If you only knew."

❖

Meike didn't know what to think when Jeanne entered the German team's half of the locker room. Her first thought was that Helen wasn't able to resume play and had decided to retire from the match. The idea left her with an odd mixture of exhilaration and disappointment. She wanted to win the match because she had earned it, not because her opponent had conceded. When Jeanne slipped a crumpled wad of paper in her hands and drew Inge and Rilla aside, however, she felt nothing but confusion.

"What—"

Meike silenced Liesel's question with a look, then unfolded the piece of paper and read the message written in Helen's familiar scrawl.

Come see me if you want to live.

Liesel stifled a gasp as she read over Meike's shoulder. "What do you think it means?" she asked in a whisper.

Meike crumpled the note in her fist to keep it safe from prying eyes. "There's only one way to find out." While Inge, Rilla, and Jeanne continued to talk, she rose from her seat and, with Liesel by her side, walked toward the Americans' half of the locker room. "You wanted to see me?" she asked as Helen, Dorothy Cheney, and Helen Hull Jacobs looked at her with equally anxious expressions.

Helen's eyes darted toward Liesel. "Do you trust her?"

Meike gripped Liesel's hand in solidarity. She and Liesel had never been exceptionally close, but she felt the fault was hers. Tennis was a solitary sport and she had been alone at the top for so long she didn't know how to let anyone in. But life was about more than tennis. She needed family. She needed friends. She needed someone to love. And here, in this room, she had found all three. "Yes, I trust her."

Helen, however, didn't appear to feel the same way. Several moments passed before she finally spoke. "I have a plan that could save your life. To make it work, you need to come with me right now. Jacobs and Dodo will cover for us while we get away."

Meike tightened her grip on Liesel's arm. "Come with you? Where?"

"London, to begin with. Swifty's at the train station now buying us tickets to Brittany so we can catch a ferry across the Channel. After we leave France, the rest is up to you. You can stay in England or emigrate to the US, Canada, or anyplace else that's out of the Nazis' reach. My friend who works for the government? He can help us secure the entry visas you'll need. You can go anywhere you want, Meike, but if you want to be safe, you have to leave before anyone knows you're gone. You have to leave now."

Helen's proposition was utterly ridiculous, incredibly dangerous, and impossibly romantic. Even though Helen hadn't revealed any details about how she planned to pull off her grand scheme, Meike felt something she hadn't felt in months: hope. Then reality quickly set in. "But I can't leave. I don't have my passport."

"Where is it?"

"In Oskar's pocket."

Helen's face fell. Meike's heart sank right along with it. Then Liesel spoke up. "I can get it for you."

"How?" Meike asked.

"I have my ways." Liesel flashed a melancholy smile. "Wait here. I shall return shortly."

"How do you know she won't tell him what we have in mind?" Helen asked skeptically as she watched Liesel leave. "How do you know she won't bring him and his friends back with her? If she does, we could all end up in jail."

Meike carefully considered the situation. Liesel was engaged to Oskar and pregnant with his child. Why would she betray him in order to help her? "Because if the situation were reversed, I would do everything in my power to help her. I choose to believe she would do the same for me."

"You're a better woman than I am." Helen took Meike's hands in hers. "Then again, I've always known that."

Time seemed to crawl by as Meike waited for Liesel to return with her passport in hand or Oskar and his henchmen in tow. She sat down hard as her legs threatened to give way. "This will be so hard on my family. I didn't get a chance to say good-bye to them."

Helen squeezed her hand. "You'll see them again someday. I promise."

Meike stared at her. Helen looked the same, but she seemed different somehow. "You've changed. You've...grown."

"No," Helen said, "I grew up. And if you'll have me, I want to grow old with you. What do you say?"

Meike felt her eyes fill with tears. "Yes. Yes. A thousand times, yes."

Helen kissed her hard. Meike returned the kiss with equal fervor.

Jacobs, who also preferred the company of women, cleared her throat. "Careful, you two. Save some for later."

Everyone started when Liesel ran back into the room. Meike held her breath for a moment as she waited for Liesel to either rescue her or condemn her. Liesel pulled Meike's passport from the folds of her jacket. "I got it."

"But how?"

"I have a cousin who's a magician. He taught me sleight of hand after one of his performances. Thanks to Enno's lessons, I picked Oskar's pocket while he was introducing me to some of his friends in the cabinet."

Meike blew out a breath, then kissed Liesel on both cheeks and clutched the passport with grateful hands. "Won't you come, too? You won't be safe once Oskar discovers you helped me escape."

"He's a good man, Meike, not the monster you think he is."

"Has he told you what he did to me when he took me to Dachau?"

"No," Liesel said with downcast eyes, "but I'm sure he was only following orders. I love him, Meike. I know his heart. I can change him. I know you don't believe that, but I do."

"We believe what we choose to believe."

"And I choose to believe in Oskar. I have to, for my sake as well as the baby's."

"Be safe." Meike placed a hand on Liesel's stomach, certain she would never see Liesel or her unborn baby again. "Both of you."

Liesel placed her hands over Meike's. "Every night before she goes to bed, I shall tell her stories about what an honor it was to play alongside you."

Meike gave Liesel three hugs. One for her mother, one for her father, and one for her brother. "When you see them, tell them…" Her voice broke and she couldn't finish.

"I won't have to say a word. They shall already know."

Meike hugged her again and held fast, unable to trade one uncertain future for another.

Helen placed a gentle hand on her shoulder. "Come on, champ," she said softly. "We've got to go."

Jacobs wheeled a half-empty linen cart toward them. Without bothering to change out of their sweat-dampened tennis clothes, Meike and Helen climbed into the cart. Jacobs and Dodo covered them with towels and piled more on top. A few minutes later, Meike felt the cart begin to move. Then she heard a man's voice say, "I'll take it from here."

"His name's Paul Lanier," Helen said in a low voice barely above a whisper. "He's the one I was telling you about."

"We're about to enter the hallway," Meike heard Paul say. "Please be as quiet as you can until I give you the okay."

Meike's pulse pounded in her ears as Paul slowly made his way across the grounds. She waited for the cart to be stopped and examined. She waited to be returned to Dachau. This time for good. Fear of discovery left a metallic taste in her mouth. Rich and coppery like dried blood.

"It's okay," Helen whispered as she stroked Meike's face. "We're almost home."

Home. How could such a small word hold such infinite possibility?

Meike heard the buzz of the milling crowd. A crowd that was waiting to see the resumption of a match she and Helen wouldn't finish.

The cart lurched to a stop. Meike froze, waiting to hear German-accented voices barking orders and guns being cocked in readiness. She blinked as the towels were plucked away to reveal the bright sun that had finally manage to burn its way through the clouds.

"Quickly now," Paul said. "The car is waiting."

Meike and Helen climbed out of the cart and ran through the bowels of the stadium to the motor car waiting just outside the gates. They climbed in the backseat while Paul joined Swifty Anderson in the front.

"I picked up your luggage from your hotel," Swifty said as he punched the gas. "You can change clothes after you board the train. You leave in twenty minutes."

"Whose car is this?" Helen asked.

"Don't ask me, kid. I liberated it from a guy who thought I was a parking attendant. I'll make sure to leave the keys in it so he can have it back when I'm done."

"How can I ever thank you, Mr. Anderson?"

"This was all her idea. Don't thank me." He jerked a thumb in Helen's direction. "Thank her."

Meike turned to the woman who had risked her own life in order to save hers. "I have a feeling I will be thanking you every day for the rest of our lives."

"Having you by my side will be thanks enough." Helen's kiss was filled with expectation and the promise of a future they would now be able to share. Together and without fear.

They reached the train station in a matter of minutes. After they boarded and entered their private car, the interminable wait for the train to leave the station began. Meike looked out the window, scanning the platform for potential pursuers.

"Where will you settle?" Paul asked as the train's whistle blew and the wheels finally began to move. "What will you do?"

"I don't know. I haven't had time to give it much thought. I'm still too busy looking over my shoulder. I won't be able to truly relax until we board the ferry and set sail for England."

"Relax," Swifty said. "Take a load off. The world is your oyster now. Stick with me. I'll make you a mint on the pro tour. Both of you. Picture it. A fifty-city tour. Six-figure contracts. I can see the posters now. Big, bold print begging crowds to come see the finale of the best match that never was. They'll be lining up down the street to buy tickets. A moment like this calls for champagne. Let me see if I can round some up."

"I could have beaten you today, you know," Helen said after Swifty left to find the bar.

"I know." Meike rested her head on Helen's shoulder as exhaustion and relief threatened to overwhelm her. "But if Swifty gets his way, you will have plenty of opportunities for a rematch."

Helen gently pulled the ribbon from Meike's hair and pressed a kiss to the top of her head. "You've got a date."

Swifty returned a few minutes later with a bottle of champagne on ice. "What shall we drink to?" he asked after he popped the cork and poured four glasses. "To fast cars?"

"To family and friends," Paul said.

"To freedom," Helen said.

Meike raised her glass, grateful for all four. "I'll drink to that."

EPILOGUE

May 1, 1946
Rheinsteifel, Germany

Helen stared out the window of the speeding taxi as she tried to see the view through Meike's eyes. The ravaged countryside bore little resemblance to the jaw-dropping beauty she remembered from her last visit eight long years ago. Deep craters dotted the landscape, brutal reminders of five years' worth of Allied bombing raids over German soil. Most of the homes were intact, but some of the historic buildings she recalled so fondly were nothing more than burned-out shells.

When the taxi neared what had once been one of her favorite haunts, Meike smiled for the first time since they had set sail from New York. "Look," she said, pointing to Brunhilde's Bakery. "It's still there."

Helen placed a hand on Meike's knee. "Tomorrow morning, perhaps we could stroll into town for some apple strudel and a cup of coffee just like old times."

"Yes," Meike said with a hint of sorrow. "Just like old times."

Anxiety rolled off Meike in waves as the cab drew ever closer to her ancestral home. The castle looked fine from a distance, but how much damage had time and war inflicted on it and the people inside its walls?

Meike hadn't seen her family since that fateful day in Paris in June 1938. When Helen had asked her to come away with her and Meike had left without looking back. So much had changed since that day.

They, like Swifty had promised, had grown rich barnstorming the United States on the professional tennis tour. Amateur competition, however, had been put on hold as dozens of players put down their racquets in order to take up arms, Helen Hull Jacobs included. Perhaps inspired by her role in springing Meike from the Nazis in Paris, Jacobs had served as a commander in the US Navy's intelligence department, one of only five women to achieve the rank. Oskar Henkel had been killed during the war, leaving Liesel a widow, though Helen didn't mourn his loss. Meike's brother, Michael, meanwhile, had been drafted into the German army, but he had chosen to flee to England rather than serve. He had pledged his support to the Allies and joined forces with Alan Turing, the British mathematician whose Enigma machine solved the German military's "unbreakable" code and helped turn the tide of the war. Michael continued to live in London and he and his wife, Lily, were expecting their first child in a few short months.

"The wheel of life," Helen said. "Once it starts to spin, you never know if you're going to hit the jackpot or crap out."

"Lady Luck has treated us pretty well, don't you think?"

"She's paid off in spades." Helen brought Meike's hand to her lips. "Every day with you is like a dream come true."

"This day," Meike said when the cab pulled to a stop in front of Castle von Bismarck and she saw her parents waiting for her on the front steps, "is better than anything I have ever imagined."

Meike jumped out of the car and ran into her parents' arms. Helen's heart filled with joy as she watched the tear-filled reunion she had once feared would never come to pass.

"Thank you for this," Max said as he pumped her hand. "Thank you for keeping Meike safe all these years and for bringing her back to us now."

"The pleasure was mine."

Katja finally released Meike and turned to Helen, who flinched involuntarily. The last time she and Katja had encountered each other, Katja had greeted her with bitter words and a slap across the face. This time, though, Katja's tone was gentle as she opened her arms and drew Helen into them. She said only two words, but they were enough to reduce Helen to tears. "Welcome home."

Helen had spent more than half her life trying to convince herself she didn't need to have a family that loved and respected her. That money could buy the happiness she'd never had. Now that she had more money than she could ever hope to spend, she realized it meant nothing without the love of the woman at her side. The woman with whom she had shared joy as well as pain. The woman she knew she could count on to remain in her corner through good times as well as bad.

Meike dried Helen's eyes. "Are you all right, my love?"

"I'm fine, darling," Helen insisted. "Because I have you."

Meike kissed her, then took her arm and led her inside. Led her to the place it had taken Helen almost thirty years and several thousand miles to find. Meike led her home.

About the Author

Yolanda Wallace is not a professional writer, but she plays one in her spare time. Her love of travel and adventure has helped her pen the globe-spanning novels *In Medias Res*, *Rum Spring*, *Lucky Loser*, the Lambda Award-winning *Month of Sundays*, and *Murphy's Law*. Her short stories have appeared in multiple anthologies including *Romantic Interludes 2: Secrets* and *Women of the Dark Streets*. She and her partner live in beautiful coastal Georgia, where they are parents to four children of the four-legged variety—a boxer and three cats.

Books Available from Bold Strokes Books

Break Point by Yolanda Wallace. In a world readying for war, can love find a way? (978-1-62639-5-688)

Countdown by Julie Cannon. Can two strong-willed, powerful women overcome their differences to save the lives of seven others and begin a life they never imagined together? (978-1-62639-4-711)

Heart of the Liliko'i by Dena Hankins. Secrets, sabotage, and grisly human remains stall construction on an ancient Hawaiian burial ground, but the sexual connection between Kerala and Ravi keeps building toward a volcanic explosion. (978-1-62639-5-565)

Keep Hold by Michelle Grubb. Claire knew some things should be left alone and some rules should never be broken, but the most forbidden, well, they are the most tempting. (978-1-62639-5-022)

The Courage to Try by C.A. Popovich. Finding love is worth getting past the fear of trying. (978-1-62639-5-282)

The Time Before Now by Missouri Vaun. Vivian flees a disastrous affair, embarking on an epic, transformative journey to escape her past, until destiny introduces her to Ida, who helps her rediscover trust, love and hope. (978-1-62639-4-469)

Twisted Whispers by Sheri Lewis Wohl. Betrayal, lies, and secrets—whispers of a friend lost to darkness. Can a reluctant psychic set things right or will an evil soul destroy those she loves? (978-1-62639-4-391)

Deadly Medicine by Jaime Maddox. Dr. Ward Thrasher's life is in turmoil. Her partner Jess has left her, and her job puts her in the path of a murderous physician who has Jess in his sights. (978-1-62639-4-247)

New Beginnings by KC Richardson. Can the connection and attraction between Jordan Roberts and Kirsten Murphy be enough for Jordan to trust Kirsten with her heart? (978-1-62639-4-506)

Officer Down by Erin Dutton. Can two women who've made careers out of being there for others in crisis find the strength to need each other? (978-1-62639-4-230)

Reasonable Doubt by Carsen Taite. Just when Sarah and Ellery think they've left dangerous careers behind, a new case sets them—and their hearts—on a collision course. (978-1-62639-4-421)

Tarnished Gold by Ann Aptaker. Cantor Gold must outsmart the Law, outrun New York's dockside gangsters, outplay a shady art dealer, his lover, and a beautiful curator, and stay out of a killer's gun sights. (978-1-62639-4-261)

The Renegade by Amy Dunne. Post-apocalyptic survivors Alex and Evelyn secretly find love while held captive by a deranged cult, but when their relationship is discovered, they must fight for their freedom—or die trying. (978-1-62639-4-278)

Thrall by Barbara Ann Wright. Four women in a warrior society must work together to lift an insidious curse while caught between their own desires, the will of their peoples, and an ancient evil. (978-1-62639-4-377)

White Horse in Winter by Franci McMahon. Love between two women collides with the inner poison of a closeted horse trainer in the green hills of Vermont. (978-1-62639-4-292)

The Chameleon by Andrea Bramhall. Two old friends must work through a web of lies and deceit to find themselves again, but in the search they discover far more than they ever went looking for. (978-1-62639-363-9)

Side Effects by VK Powell. Detective Jordan Bishop and Dr. Neela Sahjani must decide if it's easier to trust someone with your heart or your life as they face threatening protestors, corrupt politicians, and their increasing attraction. (978-1-62639-364-6)

Autumn Spring by Shelley Thrasher. Can Bree and Linda, two women in the autumn of their lives, put their hearts first and find the love they've never dared seize? (978-1-62639-365-3)

Warm November by Kathleen Knowles. What do you do if the one woman you want is the only one you can't have? (978-1-62639-366-0)

In Every Cloud by Tina Michele. When she finally leaves her shattered life behind, is Bree strong enough to salvage the remaining pieces of her heart and find the place where it truly fits? (978-1-62639-413-1)

Rise of the Gorgon by Tanai Walker. When independent Internet journalist Elle Pharell goes to Kuwait to investigate a veteran's mysterious suicide, she hires Cassandra Hunt, an interpreter with a covert agenda. (978-1-62639-367-7)

Crossed by Meredith Doench. Agent Luce Hansen returns home to catch a killer and risks everything to revisit the unsolved murder of her first girlfriend and confront the demons of her youth. (978-1-62639-361-5)

Making a Comeback by Julie Blair. Music and love take center stage when jazz pianist Liz Randall tries to make a comeback with the help of her reclusive, blind neighbor, Jac Winters. (978-1-62639-357-8)

Soul Unique by Gun Brooke. Self-proclaimed cynic Greer Landon falls for Hayden Rowe's paintings and the young woman shortly after, but will Hayden, who lives with Asperger syndrome, trust her and reciprocate her feelings? (978-1-62639-358-5)

The Price of Honor by Radclyffe. Honor and duty are not always black and white—and when self-styled patriots take up arms against the government, the price of honor may be a life. (978-1-62639-359-2)

Mounting Evidence by Karis Walsh. Lieutenant Abigail Hargrove and her mounted police unit need to solve a murder and protect wetland biologist Kira Lovell during the Washington State Fair. (978-1-62639-343-1)

Threads of the Heart by Jeannie Levig. Maggie and Addison Rae-McInnis share a love and a life, but are the threads that bind them together strong enough to withstand Addison's restlessness and the seductive Victoria Fontaine? (978-1-62639-410-0)

Sheltered Love by MJ Williamz. Boone Fairway and Grey Dawson—two women touched by abuse—overcome their pasts to find happiness in each other. (978-1-62639-362-2)

Asher's Out by Elizabeth Wheeler. Asher Price's candid photographs capture the truth, but when his success requires exposing an enemy, Asher discovers his only shot at happiness involves revealing secrets of his own. (978-1-62639-411-7)

The Ground Beneath by Missouri Vaun. An improbable barter deal involving a hope chest and dinners for a month places lovely Jessica Walker distractingly in the way of Sam Casey's bachelor lifestyle. (978-1-62639-606-7)

Hardwired by C.P. Rowlands. Award-winning teacher Clary Stone, and Leefe Ellis, manager of the homeless shelter for small children, stand together in a part of Clary's hometown that she never knew existed. (978-1-62639-351-6)

No Good Reason by Cari Hunter. A violent kidnapping in a Peak District village pushes Detective Sanne Jensen and lifelong friend Dr. Meg Fielding closer, just as it threatens to tear everything apart. (978-1-62639-352-3)

Romance by the Book by Jo Victor. If Cam didn't keep disrupting her life, maybe Alex could uncover the secret of a century-old love story, and solve the greatest mystery of all—her own heart. (978-1-62639-353-0)

Death's Doorway by Crin Claxton. Helping the dead can be deadly: Tony may be listening to the dead, but she needs to learn to listen to the living. (978-1-62639-354-7)

Searching for Celia by Elizabeth Ridley. As American spy novelist Dayle Salvesen investigates the mysterious disappearance of her ex-lover, Celia, in London, she begins questioning how well she knew Celia—and how well she knows herself. (978-1-62639-356-1)

The 45th Parallel by Lisa Girolami. Burying her mother isn't the worst thing that can happen to Val Montague when she returns to the woodsy but peculiar town of Hemlock, Oregon. (978-1-62639-342-4)

A Royal Romance by Jenny Frame. In a country where class still divides, can love topple the last social taboo and allow Queen Georgina and Beatrice Elliot, a working class girl, their happy ever after? (978-1-62639-360-8)

Bouncing by Jaime Maddox. Basketball Coach Alex Dalton has been bouncing from woman to woman, because no one ever held her interest, until she meets her new assistant, Britain Dodge. (978-1-62639-344-8)

Same Time Next Week by Emily Smith. A chance encounter between Alex Harris and the beautiful Michelle Masters leads to a whirlwind friendship, and causes Alex to question everything she's ever known—including her own marriage. (978-1-62639-345-5)

All Things Rise by Missouri Vaun. Cole rescues a striking pilot who crash-lands near her family's farm, setting in motion a chain of events that will forever alter the course of her life. (978-1-62639-346-2)

Riding Passion by D. Jackson Leigh. Mount up for the ride through a sizzling anthology of chance encounters, buried desires, romantic surprises, and blazing passion. (978-1-62639-349-3)

Love's Bounty by Yolanda Wallace. Lobster boat captain Jake Myers stopped living the day she cheated death, but meeting greenhorn Shy Silva stirs her back to life. (978-1-62639-334-9)

Just Three Words by Melissa Brayden. Sometimes the one you want is the one you least suspect. Accountant Samantha Ennis has her ordered life disrupted when heartbreaker Hunter Blair moves into her trendy Soho loft. (978-1-62639-335-6)

Lay Down the Law by Carsen Taite. Attorney Peyton Davis returns to her Texas roots to take on big oil and the Mexican Mafia, but will her investigation thwart her chance at true love? (978-1-62639-336-3)

Playing in Shadow by Lesley Davis. Survivor's guilt threatens to keep Bryce trapped in her nightmare world unless Scarlet's love can pull her out of the darkness and back into the light. (978-1-62639-337-0)

Soul Selecta by Gill McKnight. Soul mates are hell to work with. (978-1-62639-338-7)

The Revelation of Beatrice Darby by Jean Copeland. Adolescence is complicated, but Beatrice Darby is about to discover how impossible it can seem to a lesbian coming of age in conservative 1950s New England. (978-1-62639-339-4)

Twice Lucky by Mardi Alexander. For firefighter Mackenzie James and Dr. Sarah Macarthur, there's suddenly a whole lot more in life to understand, to consider, to risk...someone will need to fight for her life. (978-1-62639-325-7)

Shadow Hunt by L.L. Raand. With young to raise and her Pack under attack, Sylvan, Alpha of the wolf Weres, takes on her greatest challenge when she determines to uncover the faceless enemies known as the Shadow Lords. A Midnight Hunters novel. (978-1-62639-326-4)

Heart of the Game by Rachel Spangler. A baseball writer falls for a single mom, but can she ever love anything as much as she loves the game? (978-1-62639-327-1)

Getting Lost by Michelle Grubb. Twenty-eight days, thirteen European countries, a tour manager fighting attraction, and an accused murderer: Stella and Phoebe's journey of a lifetime begins here. (978-1-62639-328-8)

Prayer of the Handmaiden by Merry Shannon. Celibate priestess Kadrian must defend the kingdom of Ithyria from a dangerous enemy and ultimately choose between her duty to the Goddess and the love of her childhood sweetheart, Erinda. (978-1-62639-329-5)

boldstrokesbooks.com

Bold Strokes Books
Quality and Diversity in LGBTQ Literature

victory EDITIONS

Drama

MATINEE BOOKS

i

SCI-FI

E-BOOKS

MYSTERY

HE erotica

BSB SOLILOQUY

EROTICA

YOUNG ADULT

BS BOLD STROKES BOOKS

LIBERTY EDITION

Romance

W·E·B·S·T·O·R·E
PRINT AND EBOOKS